D1524388

LYNCH LAW

**Center Point
Large Print**

**This Large Print Book carries the
Seal of Approval of N.A.V.H.**

LYNCH LAW

LAURAN PAINE

CENTER POINT PUBLISHING
THORNDIKE, MAINE • USA

BOLINDA PUBLISHING
MELBOURNE • AUSTRALIA

This Center Point Large Print edition is published in the year 2004 by arrangement with Golden West Literary Agency.

This Bolinda Large Print edition is published in the year 2004 by arrangement with Golden West Literary Agency.

The text of this Large Print edition is unabridged. In other aspects, this book may vary from the original edition. Printed in Thailand. Set in 16-point Times New Roman type by Bill Coskrey and Gary Socquet.

US ISBN 1-58547-387-1
BC ISBN 1-74093-218-8

U.S. Library of Congress Cataloging-in-Publication Data.

Paine, Lauran.
    Lynch law / Lauran Paine.--Center Point large print ed.
        p. cm.
    ISBN 1-58547-387-1 (lib. bdg. : alk. paper)
    1. Lynching--Fiction. 2. Large type books. I. Title.

PS3566.A34L95 2004
813'.54--dc22

                                                        2003018620

Australian Cataloguing-in-Publication.

Paine, Lauran.
Lynch law / Lauran Paine.
1740932188
1. Large print books.
2. Lynching--Fiction.
3. Western stories.
I. Title.
813.54

British Cataloguing-in-Publication is available from the British Library.

ONE

T HE MOOD OF A TOWN, its undertones and currents and sustaining thoughts strike clearest upon strangers. The aura of village byways go into a man touching his receptive nerve-ends, bringing on a judgment of the place before he knows names or faces or events.

Particularly is this true if the stranger's business calls him to strange places where trouble is, or has been, or is impending.

Strife is a thing that roils the air on a breathless day. It is a thing that sours the darkness of a quiet night and reaches with hooked, steel fingernails to invisibly scratch the soft parts of a man's awareness. No matter how peaceful a town appears to be or how languid its inhabitants, the aftermath of trouble, or the foretaste of it, or its solid presence in the present, are there for the newcomer to scent and feel.

That was how the cowtown of Plume, Montana Territory, received Phil Gleeson on a gentle spring day with an azure sky and a rolling land merging far out in a ruggedly beautiful and mountainous setting, when he rode in tired and dusty from the winding heights of the Bitterroots.

It greeted him with a layer of leashed violence strong enough to be almost a physical force. He picked it up at the edge of Plume and passed along through it half way down Plume's broad main thoroughfare as far as *Banning's Livery Barn*. When he swung out and down it was

5

solid enough to lean into. It was also there in the hostler's eyes as he took Gleeson's horse and watched him swipe dust from his pants with a flailing hat.

It was in the gloomy lobby of the *Plume Hotel* where Gleeson dumped his saddlebags, took up the pen and registered for an upstairs room overlooking the roadway.

It put its hold on a man who had been nine days on the trail anticipating the pleasures of town life once more, diminishing his enthusiasm by degrees until, upstairs in the hotel room, he felt depressed and resentful and somehow cheated.

He stood to the side of the front window gazing dispassionately downward where traffic passed, where people moved in and out, across Plume's wide roadway, and where they stood here and there in little groups conversing.

Beyond Gleeson's window the grasslands flowed in a greeny way farther than a man could see. Beyond that rich carpeting were the purple-hulking, monolithic mountains with pink snowfields upon their dizzying heights. Serrated dark chunks of ageless stone cut jagged holes in the overhead sky where these necklaced peaks stood straight, or leaned, or plunged away in broken profusion, running in a mighty curve from east to west, running farther on, into the hazy west, until they formed the rough backbone of a continent.

But southward from Plume it was grassland again, flowing ocean-like down through a gigantic concave basin, onward through other states and other territories until, thwarted by another forming upthrust of black-cut mountains, it broke outward east and west.

There was nothing in Montana Territory which had been conceived upon a small scale; there was nothing here possessing the polish or the stability of the astringent east. Montana still had its hold-out Indians, leftovers from another time. It had its lawless and its lawlessness. It also had its lawmen like U.S. Deputy Marshal Phil Gleeson, standing up there knee-sprung, building his brown-paper cigarette and privately thinking disgruntled thoughts about this town, the people here he would meet soon now, and the business which had sent him here all the way from Denver, headquarters of the U.S. Marshal for the Northwest Territories.

Gleeson was a deliberate, quiet and thoughtful man. Nature had punched a lot of bone and muscle down under his sun-darkened hide. He was heavily flat and angular with light brown eyes, light brown hair, strong features and a barrel chest. His lips were thin and long and compressed from long habit. His hands were big and scarred with the tip of a finger missing off his right hand—caught between the saddlehorn and the lariat when Gleeson had had fourteen hundred pounds of fighting Durham bull on the other end of that lariat.

He read each sign across the road beginning with *Patterson's Apothecary Shop* and ending with *Corbett's Saloon.* He particularly read the large black legend painted above the little overhang upon a solid log building southward and below his hotel room. *SHERIFF* that legend said, which made big Phil Gleeson grunt, because there were no incorporated counties in Montana Territory. Not that it made any difference; statehood was a solid dream with Montanans; they created counties and cities and towns so that the day statehood arrived, they'd be all ready for it.

Gleeson killed his smoke. He had memorized every store-front down there, every byway leading into Plume and out of it, every dog-trot between buildings. He knew Plume a heap better than it knew him, so now he would go make an acquaintance. The sheriff.

Back downstairs again Gleeson felt that gloominess, that aura of leashed violence again. He stepped out into the roadway, scuffed over to the far side, stepped up and swung southward as far as that little, separate log building which was combination sheriff's office and local jail. He entered, filling the door, blocking out all daylight until he'd stepped clear, swung his tawny gaze at the balding man seated drowsily at an ancient desk, and dispassionately nodded.

This lawman's name would be Riley. Terry Riley. Gleeson remembered this much from the telegram he'd received four hundred miles away, up at Lodgepole.

Riley had a shoe-button nose, merry blue eyes that seemed to laugh—like now—when instead they were actually shrewdly taking a man's measure, and bandy, bowed legs supporting an over-balanced upper torso of solid muscle.

Gleeson fished in a pocket, drew forth his deputy marshal's shield-type badge, tossed it upon Riley's desk and leaned upon the wall crossing one leg over the other leg at the ankle, waiting; studying Sheriff Terry Riley and waiting.

"Well," said Riley, eyeing that badge. "Well now. I hardly expected you for a week yet. Denver's a long ways from Plume and the trains ain't entirely reliable."

"I wasn't far off," said Gleeson. "Denver wired me to ride over and look in."

Gleeson had said this casually. He had not meant it to sound belittling but he instantly saw that Sheriff Riley chose to interpret it this way. Riley's merry eyes became less merry. His mastiff jaw jutted and he hardened his face toward the deputy marshal.

"It'll take more than a little lookin' in, I'm afraid, Mister Marshal. In fact it might even take more than just one federal lawman. You see, me bucko, this is a raw, rough land for a fact, and strangers—even fine upstandin' ones with lashed down guns on their hips and silver marshals' shields in their pockets—are as welcome as cholera to some folks hereabouts."

Gleeson regarded Riley's mildly antagonistic expression. He hadn't meant to rub the local lawman the wrong way. Still, if Riley had a thin skin that would be Riley's concern, not his. He wouldn't apologize, regardless; once you started apologizing to thin-skinned people you never had time for anything else.

"My orders were to look in. That's what I rode this far for and that's what I figure to do, Sheriff. If someone's got it in for strangers. . . ." Gleeson lifted his shoulders and let them fall. "Now how about giving me some facts?"

Riley's pugnaciousness came up. He looked up at Gleeson making no attempt to hide this when he said, "Deputy; you're a pretty big man, but we got a lot of big men in this country."

Phil made a slashing gesture of quick temper, quick

impatience, with one big hand. "Never mind the facts of life," he said, taking a dislike to the massively-built, bandy-legged sheriff. "Let's have it; what's the trouble here in Plume?"

Riley turned a rusty colour, he snapped his lips harshly closed and firepoints shone from his eyes. For a moment he was quite silent.

This one, Gleeson told himself, is one of those deceptively smiling ones that operate on a short fuse. Well; it takes all kinds and when a man's dog-tired he doesn't care about humouring folks.

When Riley spoke again his words were carefully enunciated and fell like steel balls striking glass. "There was a killing, deputy; a cowboy named Bannister shot a cowboy named Furth. That started it."

"Where is Bannister?"

Riley jerked his head sideways. "Out back in one of my cells, deputy, locked up."

"All right; go on."

"Thanks," grated Riley sarcastically. "Thanks a lot. Like I was sayin', Chet Bannister killed Dean Furth in Jack Corbett's place down the road. That was a week ago. Now, we get a circuit rider through here to attend court trials once a month. He was here four days before Bannister shot Furth, which means he won't be back for about another three weeks, and meanwhile the feeling's been mounting against Chet Bannister." Riley leaned back as though relishing the sound of his voice or the impact of his words, or both.

"Ordinarily a killing wouldn't make such a stir. We've had other shooting scrapes in Plume, but Bannister's a sort of fiddle-footed cuss who rides for the cow outfits until he's flush, then sits around Corbett's place drinkin' an' playin' cards."

"And Furth?" asked Gleeson.

Riley wickedly smiled. "He was the son of Oliver Furth, owner of the Maple Leaf ranch, which just happens to be the biggest, richest, toughest cow outfit south of Canada and west of the Missouri."

Gleeson softly sighed; this was an old, old story, the way it was shaping up. "And this Oliver Furth's standing the drinks, stirring the feelings, and organizing the lynch-lawyers."

Riley's wicked smile remained. "Sort of like that," he conceded. "A feller can't exactly blame him, can he?"

Gleeson's gaze cooled out a little toward the seated man. "That's odd," he drawled. "I always thought a lawman's job was to enforce the law, remain neutral, and avoid personal implications."

"Did you now," said Terry Riley, not the least disturbed by this admonition. He eased forward in his chair, drummed upon the desktop and said, "Funny thing about prejudices; some we develop half-grown, some we develop when we're full-grown. But some seem to be with us from birth, like shootin' down unarmed men and the like."

Riley stopped drumming and stopped wickedly smiling. He was staring straight into Gleeson's eyes blank-faced and cold to the bigger man's presence.

Gleeson returned this stare briefly, then stepped away from the wall, caught an old chair by its top, spun it one-handed and eased down across it with both large arms hooked over the back.

"Bannister shot Furth when Furth was unarmed, is that what you're saying, Sheriff?"

"That's what I'm sayin', deputy."

"Why?"

"Over a girl."

Gleeson lowered his head, put his chin upon those hooked big arms and looked saturnine. "A lousy lovers' quarrel and I have to spend nine days in the saddle," he growled. "Tell me something, Sheriff; whose girl was she, Bannister's or Furth's?"

"Bannister's. He was married to her."

"Well; that complicates it a little but it doesn't change the facts, does it? Shooting unarmed people is murder— even in an out-of-the-way place like Plume."

"Listen deputy, if you don't like this town I'll be glad to show you the—"

"Rope it, Riley," growled Gleeson pushing up off the chair. "I don't like any town that stinks of trouble a mile out before you ride on in. I don't like 'em because I've seen my share of dust watered down with blood in places like this one—and for no better reason than you've just given me."

Gleeson stepped to the doorway, filled it with his bulk and turned. Riley was shrewdly watching him from over at the desk.

"Nine lousy days in the saddle—for this!"

Gleeson passed on out onto the plankwalk, stood a moment running his disillusioned eyes up and down Plume's central thoroughfare, felt the quick, good warmth of spring sunlight beat against him, and decided to visit *Corbett's Saloon* to cut some of the trail scorch out of his pipes.

Behind him, watching Gleeson's big stride carry the deputy marshal southward, Terry Riley came out to lean and look and slowly smile his wicked smile again. One thing about those deputy U.S. marshals; they always acted as though the troubles which brought them, were a lot less worthwhile than the way they liked their trouble. Well; some men lived and learned and some just lived.

TWO

J ACK CORBETT had come to the Territory six years before; some said he'd come out of Texas two jumps and a holler ahead of a posse. But whatever had induced him to settle in Plume, he had been as exemplary a citizen since opening his place as saloon owners can be.

Jack was a man of middle-height, tough and durable and quick-tempered. He was, the oldtimers opined, somewhat like an Indian; he was gregarious, generous to a fault at times, sometimes expansively good-humoured and sometimes a cyclone of violence. The difference between Jack Corbett and an Indian was that with Jack people could tell when he was going to explode. His temper was violent but it was predictable. Some things struck sparks from Jack; when that happened he would rush in swinging.

He was not a tall man. In fact he was an inch or two under average height. But he had the shoulders, arms and chest of a blacksmith. He also had the scarred face and flattened nose of a fighter. Still, he was not a bad looking man, with his straightforward blue eyes, his mouth-full of large white teeth, and his fierce dragoon moustache with its wickedly up-curving outer ends. He had a smile that could disarm people and a booming laugh that could instantly lift the spirits of the weariest trail-hand.

But Jack didn't smile when the big stranger entered his place, for like the rest of Plume he'd seen this man ride in all travel stained, and he'd heard how this stranger had registered at the hotel, then had spent an hour over at Terry Riley's jailhouse, and with the town in its present mood as a result of the killing in his saloon, Jack Corbett could sense that this large, easy-moving man meant trouble. There had been a few men in his place earlier who'd predicted that the stranger was one of those itinerant federal lawmen who came riding out of nowhere if trouble was impending. In Jack Corbett's view that was exactly what Plume *didn't* need right now—some damned federal meddler to quicken the smouldering indignation in town.

April Bannister saw the deputy marshal enter too. She had taken a job with Corbett after her husband was locked up for the very elemental reason that a girl had to eat.

April was young and quite handsome in a sulphurous, hard, and sort of disillusioned way. She had a pretty face a swelling figure and a bitter way of looking at men that, instead of repelling them as it was meant to do, excited their male instincts.

But as long as Jack Corbett was around the trail-hands

and townsmen made their sly little veiled suggestions, but they never went any farther than that because everyone knew Jack Corbett was the friend of April Bannister's husband.

It was this very friendship, which Corbett had stubbornly refused to disavow after the killing of unarmed Dean Furth, which had resulted in only these two people being in the saloon when Phil Gleeson strolled in, crossed over to the bar and gravely nodded across it at the clear-eyed and battle-scarred countenance he found there.

Corbett's unyielding stubbornness had set the entire surrounding countryside against him for remaining loyal to Bannister. And as he might have expected, the moment he gave employment to Bannister's young wife, the talk turned slyly knowing.

"What'll it be?" Corbett asked, looking straight over at Gleeson, his face expressionless, his eyes two wet stones in puckered surroundings.

"Ale," replied Gleeson. "Ale and a little help."

Gleeson fished out his shield, held it briefly in his palm then returned it to his pocket. Corbett looked, reached under the bar for Gleeson's drink, set it upon the bartop and raised his eyes in a dark look. "All we sell here is liquor, mister."

Gleeson put a coin beside his untouched glass and nodded. "I know; that's all they ever sell in saloons. I'm not buyin' anything anyway, Corbett—you are Corbett aren't you?"

"I am."

"And the young lady standing at the far end of the

bar strainin' her ears—she'd be April Bannister wouldn't she?"

"She would."

Gleeson stopped speaking. He considered the ale for a moment, lifted it, drank and set the glass down again. He smiled.

"Not bad, Corbett. Not bad at all. That's the first drink I've had in nine days; it sort of settles m'stomach."

"Now that your stomach's settled," stated Jack Corbett evenly, "why don't you settle the other end of you across your saddle and ride back wherever you came from, deputy?"

Gleeson's eyes lifted and grew still. "You figure that would help?"

"I think so, yes."

"You're sitting on a powder keg, Corbett. This whole lousy town's perched up there with you, and I think a man named Oliver Furth is trying to light the fuse under you."

Corbett leaned over the bar. "Let me tell you something about this town, deputy. You're a stranger here; all you know is what Terry Riley may have told you, and perhaps what you've sensed."

"That's right. Have I missed something else?"

Corbett ignored the question. "I expect you've seen lynch-law work before, deputy. I have. It follows a pattern; folks get fired up; they're brimming with indignation. They brood and after a while they either go hang someone or they don't. That's the way things are here right now; folks are broodin'. They're trying to make up their minds. The longer they think about hangin' Chet

16

Bannister the less likely they are to ever do it. It's like fighting; if a man's going to fight he doesn't talk. But if he *does* start talkin', then he won't fight."

"I see. And what you're tellin' me is that if things are left alone—folks are left to talk—they won't try to hang young Bannister."

"That's part of what I'm telling you, deputy. The other part is that just by riding into this town you've focused all the diminishing attention back upon what's just lately been beginning to die down—all this lynch-talk." Corbett straightened up off the bar. "Finish your drink," he said, looking down. "The next one is on the house."

When Gleeson obediently lifted his glass Jack Corbett twisted from the waist, jerked his head at the girl down the empty bar from Gleeson, and she dutifully started forward.

Corbett drew three glasses, solemnly set them up, pointed with his chin and said, "This is April Bannister, wife to the feller Riley's got locked up at his jailhouse."

Gleeson looked, admired what he saw, and gravely nodded. April did not return the nod. She had a heavy underlip and smoky eyes that shone with banked fires. She simply gave Gleeson a blank acknowledgement and turned her face toward Corbett who lifted a glass, leaned down again, and stared at Gleeson over the rim.

"Here's to hell," he said, making a grim little toast with an upraised glass. "May the stay there be as pleasant as the way there."

Gleeson smiled. Those two rough men locked glances then drank. April Bannister sipped her ale, put the glass down and stood looking sullen, looking troubled and confused and not quite comprehending.

"So ride on, deputy," exclaimed Corbett quietly. "Do us all a favour."

"Furth too?" asked Gleeson.

Corbett turned his glass in its sticky little pool. "Furth," he said, speaking slowly and thoughtfully, "isn't going to get the job done."

"No?"

"No." Corbett stopped turning the glass. He looked past Gleeson out the barroom front window to the sun-lighted roadway beyond. "Furth has spent twenty years walking over folks to build his cow empire. He's wealthy and he's powerful, yes, but his hands are a little soiled, deputy, and that's what folks remember."

"Sheriff Riley thinks he might get the job done, Corbett, using influence and money—mostly money."

Corbett gently wagged his head. "Deputy; a saloon man gets to know his customers. I know how the people hereabouts feel towards Oliver Furth. They'll listen to him; they'll drink when he sets 'em up, but they only smile when he tells 'em what to do."

Gleeson raised his eyebrows. "Then how come this town to feel like a time-bomb?"

"I didn't say there aren't plenty who want to lynch Chet. I said Furth won't stampede 'em into it. I also said your being here brings the thing to a head, deputy. If you ride on they'll go back to mulling it over. If you don't ride on. . . ." Corbett lifted his shoulders and dropped them.

Phil Gleeson emptied his glass, pushed it aside, turned and put his assessing gaze upon April Bannister. She stood there looking younger than she was, looking resentful and cynical. He could understand any man's physical attraction to her, but now he began to wonder what kind of a man her husband was. He thought he knew and this knowledge made him feel old. Bannister would be youthful and full of the fires of the young and the immature; the animal fires that asked nothing more of a mate than to have the voluptuousness of this girl. Gleeson sighed; it was hell, sometimes, being thirty-five years old and to have seen so much of life.

"Tell me about the fight," he said, speaking to Corbett but still studying the girl. "Furth was unarmed they say."

Corbett removed their emptied glasses, dumped them into a bucket under the bar and muttered: "They say."

Gleeson's gaze swivelled back. He watched Corbett fussing under his bar, head lowered, eyes unreadable. "Well; wasn't he unarmed?"

"Deputy; Dean Furth was a troublemaker. I've known him ever since I been in this town and never have I seen him unarmed."

"Did he, or did he not, have a gun-belt around him the day he was killed by Bannister?"

Corbett shook his head, his expression turning wry. "No sir, he had no gun-belt around him." Corbett paused, put both broad hands upon his bartop, and said, "He very seldom ever wore a gun-belt, deputy. He was one of those sly ones who carried a Colt Lightning in his belt under his coat or in his coat pocket. I know—so does everyone else around here—that's how he operated. And I've seen him stand there grinnin' at some drifter or some other unsuspectin' cowboy with his right hand in his coat pocket, tryin' to force a fight with some cuss who wouldn't fight Dean because they couldn't see any weapon on him."

Gleeson faintly frowned. "A hide-out-gunman," he muttered. "All right; the West's full of that kind too. Now tell me this: How many people were in here the night—or day—"

"It happened about suppertime."

"All right; how many folks saw this fight in the evening when Bannister killed Furth?"

"Maybe a dozen. Maybe fifteen or twenty. It was a busy night. But the thing happened pretty fast. Dean grabbed April when she came in to get Bannister. Chet called him on that and Furth started to push his right hand into his coat pocket. Bannister drew and fired—and killed him."

"And afterwards," said Gleeson, watching Corbett closely. "Who bent over Furth?"

For the first time April spoke up. She put a testy look upon Gleeson and said fiercely, "Everyone; the place was crowded. People crowded up three deep. I tried to get through to see how badly Dean was hurt and I couldn't even see him. Everyone was talking and pushing up. . . ."

April didn't complete it. She swung her head away. Gleeson looked across the bar and Corbett gravely nodded.

"That's the way it happened," he said, pulled his lips down, ran the back of one hand under his fierce dragoon moustache and gave Gleeson look for look. "You try and prove Dean *was* armed, and that someone sneaked the

20

pistol out of his pocket when he was lyin' there—and I'll bet you a good horse you never get the job done, deputy."

THREE

GLEESON HAD A BATH at the hotel. He soaked ingrained trail-dirt out of his hide until he looked as old and wrinkled and pink as a walrus. He afterwards dressed in fresh clothing, went down to a little café sandwiched between a bank and an express office, drank three cups of good coffee and ate like a horse.

Afterwards he bought a Mexican cigar, strolled out onto the night-shadowed sidewalk and found a bench to sit upon while he lit up, savoured the sting and aroma of that good tobacco, and let the town of Plume go on about its business around him.

A few men entered *Corbett's Saloon*, but not many. Not nearly as many, Gleeson surmised, as had patronized the place before Furth's killing. Well; that's the way things worked out; people extolled loyalty and at the same time denounced it.

Across from Corbett's place was another saloon, *Banning's Bar.* That name rang a bell. Gleeson peered around at the livery stable sign, saw the same name there too, and concluded that whoever Banning was, he must be full of enterprise.

Sheriff Riley came by making his rounds, stopped and studied Gleeson's sprawled and comfortable position. "You don't look like a man who's got half a town talkin' about him," said the sheriff.

Gleeson removed the cigar, examined its ash, and flicked it. "Didn't know I was that much of a celebrity, Sheriff."

"Oh, you are, Gleeson, you are. Even Ab Turlock the undertaker's interested in you." Riley made his wicked smile again. "You'd be surprised who-all's interested in you."

"Oliver Furth maybe," said Gleeson softly. "And his rough-tough Maple Leaf outfit?"

Riley stepped back to lean his top-heavy frame against an overhang upright. "I feel sorry for you, deputy. This isn't as funny or as simple as you seem to think."

"Murder's never funny, Sheriff, even when it turns out that it might be only a justified killing."

Riley stiffened. His dark brows drew down. "How, justified?" he demanded. "How do you justifiably kill an unarmed man when he's—?"

"Cut it out, Sheriff," said Gleeson, looking unwaveringly across the little distance separating these two. "You knew this Furth. You knew he was a hide-out-gunman. Why didn't you mention that this afternoon when we talked?"

"He didn't have any damned gun on him when Bannister shot him. That's all I know, deputy. That's all the law needs to know."

Gleeson replaced the Mex cigar. He puffed it idly, thoughtfully, while he began to sceptically assess Terry Riley. "How much money would you say it might take to buy a man in this country, Sheriff?" he asked in a drawling way, but with his eyes hard and his jaw clamped down.

Terry Riley's shoulders rolled together. He pushed off the overhang upright and said, "Deputy; I hope you didn't mean that the way it sounded."

Neither of them said anything more. Riley, after a little while, settled back, his gaze turning bleak and sardonic. He appeared to Gleeson to be balancing something in his mind but he never formed it into words, he simply set his back to the federal officer and went along northward with his rolling, top-heavy gait.

Gleeson watched him until, in the half-light, half-shadows over by Banning's saloon upon the opposite plankwalk, he halted to talk with several riders who'd just loped in to tie up and troop forward. There were four of those cowboys and every one of them was taller than Terry Riley. They were the loose, rangy, rough looking breed of men one usually found in cowcamps from Canada to Mexico.

Then Riley walked on and the four rangy silhouettes over there pushed on into Banning's place, their spurs audible over where Gleeson sat quietly smoking, quietly sprawled, and feeling that little spark of restlessness which claims active men after a good meal and a long smoke.

The town was almost as busy after dark as it had been before. Some of the larger stores were still open for business, people passed back and forth among them, now and then exchanging words when neighbours inadvertently encountered neighbours. Riders moved in and out of alternating light and darkness, some entering Plume, some passing on out.

A late stage arrived before the express office, curling roadway dust upwards from its broad wheels. Gleeson idly watched passengers alight. A very handsome woman was the first one down. She held Gleeson's attention as she paused, threw a long look around, then gathered her skirts and struck out for the hotel. Two drummers alighted next, each with his sample-case and his carpet-bag; these two didn't give Plume a glance. They were obviously tired and hungry and disgruntled. They too headed at once for the hotel.

The last passenger was a broad, thickly-made man with a cowman's dark hat sitting back on his head and a tied-down ivory-butted sixgun lashed to his right hip. He caught a valise someone tossed him from the coach-top, stepped away and halted to swing his head in a challenging bold way, looking left and looking right.

Gleeson drew straight up over where he sat watching this passenger. He took out the cigar, formed a name upon his lips, then, instead of saying it, he said only "Damn!"

The burly man started onward toward the hotel. Gleeson rose up, sauntered through a long dark patch to where one of the lighted globes beside the hotel entrance spilled its weak, milky light over him, and stopped to lean there, his eyes drawn out narrow, his cigar jutting, and both his thumbs hooked in his shell-belt.

The stranger came on, saw Gleeson, neither faltered in his stride nor so much as batted an eyelash, passed by and disappeared into the hotel lobby.

Gleeson turned to push both shoulders against the wooden wall at his back, to look broodingly over where hostlers were changing stage-teams, and made quite a point of watching how this was done. He was still standing there, thumbs hooked, cigar jutting, eyes dead ahead, some ten minutes later when the burly big man with that ivory-stocked sixgun strolled forth, paused to look up and down the roadway, say from the corner of his mouth, "Midnight; room nine upstairs," then twist to saunter northward through the balmy night.

Gleeson ambled back to his bench, eased down there, tossed away his cigar and pursed his lips. When the U.S. Marshal himself rode all this way from Denver, one of his deputies could bet a year's pay it wasn't because he was feeling brotherly solicitude.

But it didn't make sense either; there was nothing here to draw Bill Danvers all the way from Denver: A hot-headed young fool had killed another of the same type. It was happening every day somewhere in the West. Sure; there were undercurrents; lynch-talk, a sheriff who was probably as crooked as a dog's hind leg, an anguished father named Furth and a saloonman as shrewd as he was stubborn. But these were the basic ingredients of half the cases Gleeson had been sent out on.

There was something else, then; something serious enough to make Danvers ride the coaches all the way from Denver. Or—perhaps he was just returning from somewhere else.

No. Phil Gleeson knew Bill Danvers better than that. Whenever Danvers took the measure of a town like he'd done after he alighted from that stage, he had a reason for doing so.

Gleeson stood up. Danvers being here spelled real trouble. Hell; Phil'd had hopes he could wind this other thing up within the next few days and head for home. Denver had some pretty good places for a man to relax in. Gleeson had been away four months now and he was tired of cowtowns and beaneries and hotel beds or camp-side gravel pits. He started walking northward towards Corbett's place.

From across the way at *Banning's Bar* came an abrupt outburst of banjo music and boisterous singing. Else-where, near the liverybarn's doorless wide, square opening, a number of idlers stood slouching, talking a little back and forth. Near *Patterson's Apothecary Shop* was another group of idlers. Patterson left a little blue lamp burning in his window at night; this made a pleasant little light and it helped to have that wall-bench bolted over there too; men often met there to sit in the evenings and talk, or just endlessly whittle.

Corbett's hitchrack, though, of all the racks along Plume's north-south roadway, was nearly empty. Three drowsing saddle animals drooped there, patiently waiting. They lent an air of gloominess to the saloon across from them. Gleeson noted this as he passed for-ward, got almost to Corbett's spindle-doors, was in fact beginning to veer off to his right a little, when four rangy big men stepped forth from dark places and converged.

Gleeson felt those hostile presences almost before he actually saw the men. He was not a man who had trouble with decisions, ever. These men meant him no good. They appeared to be the same four Terry Riley had briefly spoken to earlier, over in front of *Banning's Bar.*

26

In the split second it took him to make his judgement and act upon it, his vision grew very clear, his heart stepped up its pumping, a coldness grew in him and he moved.

The foremost of those converging men was near enough for Gleeson to see the fire-points in his gaze, the age-old primitive lust to battle. This man was still coming along, arms slightly forward, hands beginning to lift, to curl, when Gleeson lunged and lashed out. The shock of that powerful blow jarred Gleeson all the way to his toes. The cowboy's eyes flew wide, his jaw sagged and his head snapped back violently. He didn't stagger, he simply raised far up and went over backwards unconscious before he struck hard down, half on the plankwalk, half in the manured roadway dust.

Gleeson didn't stop. He caught the second man over the heart, doubled him over, caught him a sledging strike at the base of the skull and dropped him like a stone directly at his feet.

He half turned to face the third man, but this one, startled at the speed, at the viciousness of this slashing attack, stopped, gaped, then started rapidly backwards throwing up his hands to paw at Gleeson, to keep him off. The fourth man jumped in, mightily swung and jumped out again. His blow missed by ten inches but Gleeson felt the roiled air of it.

Gleeson swung, crouched low and settled flat down into his boots. He saw the fourth man make his second drive forward, arms swinging, breath whistling, and he hovered until the very last moment before leaping sideways, twisting and firing a big fist with all his power crowded in behind it, all his considerable heft. The pain of that blow went through Gleeson like an electric shock. His knuckles grated over bone with a meaty sound. The fourth man went fifteen feet out into the roadway before he broke over in the middle, went down flat upon his face and lay sprawled and totally unmoving. He'd been sledged below and behind the right ear.

The remaining cowboy seemed stunned, seemed totally disbelieving. He looked bewilderedly at his wrecked companions; he looked over at Phil Gleeson, who was also watching him, then he made his worst mistake of the night—he went for his gun.

Gleeson's right hand blurred in a downward dive. He whipped his body sideways. He beat that cowboy to the draw by a full two seconds. He could see terror fill the other man's face a fraction ahead of his trigger-tug. That was how fast the cowboy's mind worked; he knew ahead of that thunderous solitary gunshot that he'd been outgunned. He knew it, yet his reflexes could not keep pace with that instantaneous burst of final knowledge, then the bullet struck him square and he threw out one hand, went drunkenly backwards a step and a half and collapsed.

Jack Corbett was the first one up. Corbett had a sawed-off shotgun in his hands. His barman's apron shone palely in the night. He burst out of his saloon swinging his head and that gun from left to right.

Others came up too, but more slowly, much more cautiously. Generally, men remained out in the roadway content to peer over where those four scattered bodies lay around the rawboned, hard-breathing big federal lawman.

There was a little ripple of suppressed conversation. It ran like a gentle wind up and down Plume's roadway. A hostler walked as far as the liverybarn doorway holding up a lantern, but he walked no farther than that.

Corbett looked at Gleeson, at the downed men, put his scattergun in one hand, bent and flopped one of Gleeson's assailants over onto his back. He stared hard at that rangerider, stiffened up and spat out a name.

"Furth! Furth's Maple Leaf riders!"

Gleeson, looking ahead where crowding men stood motionlessly staring, spied a burly, iron-jawed man among them. This one had an ivory-butted sixgun tied low on his right leg.

Terry Riley pushed through looking fierce and bleak. He knelt by the shot cowboy, bent down to peer into those sightless, drying eyes, and twisted from the waist.

Gleeson caught that wintry look. "Tell me he didn't have a gun," he said to Riley, shucked the spent casing out of his revolver, plugged in a fresh one and slammed it into his hip-holster.

Riley got up, absently dusted his knees and darkly looked around, being deliberate about the way he kept his back to Gleeson.

FOUR

A T MIDNIGHT Gleeson slipped into Bill Danvers' room in his stocking feet and Danvers peered at him over the newspaper he was reading, looking caustic.

Without any kind of a greeting after four months of not

seeing one another Danvers said: "That was real clever of you, Phil. One dead and three knocked silly."

Danvers carefully folded his paper and put it aside. He leaned back in the chair he occupied, put his fingertips together and critically studied his deputy.

Gleeson's colour mounted upwards turning his sun-layered features rusty. "Did you expect me to take their shellacking without fighting back?" He asked sharply, his voice rushing at Danvers in a knife-edged way. "Not at those odds, Bill. You wouldn't have either."

"Maybe not. But then I wouldn't have ridden into this stinkin' little place with a brass band proclaiming myself a U.S. lawman, either."

"Who said I did that?" snapped Gleeson, stepping to a chair, whipping it around and dropping down upon it. "You better get the facts straight before you go jumpin' people, Bill. I had my badge in my pocket when I rode in."

"Twenty minutes after you arrived everyone knew you were a federal marshal."

"Your damned telegram said for me to contact Sheriff Terrence Riley. That's exactly what I did. Now, if anyone had verbal dysentery it was Riley, because he was the only person in Plume who knew I was a deputy U.S. marshal."

Danvers put up a hand, ran it through his curly, greying hair, and looked tired. "Well," he growled, "It's done." He said this with finality, finished scratching his head and looked back again at Gleeson. "The talk at *Banning's Bar* has it that you're here to spirit Bannister out of Plume in the night."

"The idea had occurred to me," said Gleeson.

"Well; forget it. There is a lot of feeling here against Bannister. There'll be spies all over the place from today on. You try saving Bannister's bacon, Phil, and I'll have to cart you back to Denver in a pine box."

Gleeson recalled what Jack Corbett had said about his presence bringing the trouble over Bannister to a head. He commented on this to the U.S. Marshal, but Danvers only shook his head.

"Suppose they *do* lynch Bannister," he reasoned. "How would it look in print that a U.S. deputy marshal deliberately saddled up an' rode off a day or two before Bannister got strung up?"

Gleeson crossed his legs, stared at his stockinged feet and nodded without speaking.

"No; you stay in town. As for this Riley feller—watch him like a hawk. It's possible you're right about him being a sell-out to Oliver Furth. I'm inclined to believe that myself and I've never talked to the man. The reason I believe it, with all the lynch-talk I heard at Banning's place, never once did any of those hotheads mention the possibility of Riley giving them any trouble about busting Bannister out of his jail." Danvers raised thick legs, propped them upon a tabletop and leaned back. "*Banning's Bar* is the headquarters for the pro-lynch mob. I gathered from their talk that Corbett's place across the road is where the anti-lynchers hang out."

Gleeson made a wry face. "Yeah—all three of us, Bill. Jack Corbett, Bannister's wife, and me."

Danvers smiled. "Most of your jobs find you lined up on the weak side, don't they, Phil?"

"I didn't ask for this assignment."

Danvers' smile winked out. "Don't worry, I wired for Bert McKay and Charley Barrett to get over here as fast as they can." Danvers rubbed his eyes, yawned and blinked. "Bert and Charley have been after the Morgan brothers. You've probably heard about that; it's been one hell of a chase."

Gleeson was staring hard at Danvers; an idea was firming up in his mind. "Go on," he quietly said.

"I think Furth has hired the Morgans. At least I got that notion when the grapevine had it that the Morgans suddenly cut loose from Dodge City bound up in this direction."

"This is a big territory, Bill."

"Yeah. But for now the only likely big money to be offered for three fast guns like the Morgans, centres around Plume, where a rich cowman lost a son."

Gleeson stood up, walked to the door and walked back. The Morgans were notorious killers. There were three of them—Caleb, called Cal, Moses, called Moe, and Ralph. They were will-o'-the-wisps. They were too well known to remain long in any one place. A total reward of seven thousand dollars was out for them, dead or alive. Their faces were tacked up in front of sheriffs' offices between the Nueces and the Bighorn.

"I wondered what it was brought you up here, Bill, when I saw you get off that coach tonight."

"And now you know. The only place we've consistently failed is with the Morgan brothers. If they show up here, Phil, we can't fail this time. We don't dare fail. The lousy newspapers have been raking us fore and aft for a

32

year now, and I keep getting nasty letters from Washington."

"Furth," Gleeson thoughtfully said, "must have offered a whale of a lot of money—if he really did send for the Morgans."

"I checked on this Oliver Furth before I left Denver. He's a member in good standing of the Livestock Growers Association." Danvers stood up, began unbuttoning his shirt. "He's a rich man, Phil. Rich enough to hire the Morgans, the Youngers, Frank Leslie and Tom Horn if he wanted to."

Danvers tossed aside the shirt, sat down and tugged at his boots. Gleeson began to make a cigarette. He scowled over this undertaking, eventually lit up and gazed down at his toes.

"When Bert and Charley get here the four of us can take Bannister out of town in the night, Bill."

Danvers was unbuckling his gun-belt when he answered. "Naw; I look at it like this, Phil. If we've got to use bait to have our chance at the Morgans, let's use someone like this Bannister. If he was a decent citizen I'd agree with you—but he isn't."

"Wait a minute, Bill. You're pre-judging Bannister. I'm not so damned sure that Furth killing wasn't planned."

"Planned?" said Danvers, pausing to look up. "Planned how?"

"Corbett told me in his saloon today that Dean Furth was a hide-out-gunman; that he's never known Furth to be unarmed."

"I see."

"I don't know how true that might or might not be; I haven't had a chance to talk to very many people. Just that damned sheriff, Corbett, and Bannister's wife. But I can tell you this—if Furth *was* armed, *was* going for his gun when Bannister downed him, then someone removed that gun off the body immediately, and if that's so, Bill, my guess is that someone deliberately framed Bannister for murder."

"Any ideas, Phil?"

"Listen, dammit, I just rode into this lousy town this afternoon."

Danvers shed his gun and belt, he eased down on the side of his bed wiggling his toes. "You're tired," he eventually said, "and so am I." He lingered a moment in thought, then his expression turned raffish. "But I got to hand it to you, Phil; half a day in a town and you've already killed a stupid cowboy and knocked three others senseless, got the town talkin' about you like you were some kind of a legendary figure, and no doubt by this time Oliver Furth's been told a genuine hell-roaring deputy U.S. marshal's in town to prevent a lynching."

Danvers' shrewd, grey eyes went to Gleeson's face, tartly twinkling.

"But that's enough for one day. Head out now and get some sleep. One more thing, Phil; don't contact me, I'll contact you. For as long as it's possible to do so, let's just leave things as they are; I'm a foot-loose cowman looking for land to buy. I don't know you and you don't know me."

Gleeson strolled to the door, reached for the latch and dryly said, "Thanks, Bill. Thanks a lot for all this support." He passed on out into the dark hallway, eased the door closed and padded along to his room. There, with something white lying half beneath his own door to snag Gleeson's attention, he bent, picked the folded paper up, entered his quarters and lighted a lamp.

The paper was a hastily scrawled note bearing two initials instead of a signature. J. C. Jack Corbett. The note informed Gleeson that an hour after the fight in which one of Furth's Maple Leaf riders had been killed, Oliver Furth and his foreman Dewey Porter rode into town. Corbett advised Gleeson to get out of Plume, at least for the night; he said he did not think even Oliver Furth would dare have a U.S. deputy marshal assassinated in broad daylight, but he wouldn't bet it wouldn't be tried in the dark.

Gleeson blew down the lamp-chimney plunging his room into total darkness. He paced to the window, stood off a little to one side and looked downward and across the roadway toward *Banning's Bar.* There was a crowded hitchrack over there, and although it was after one o'clock in the morning the place was brilliantly lit. The one thing which struck Gleeson now, was that, despite all the people in Banning's place, there was no music, no loud sounds of revelry, no noise at all.

He saw Sheriff Riley come out, pause to glance up and down the all but deserted roadway, then slowly and deliberately look up at the window behind which Gleeson was standing, before he ultimately went rolling southward towards his jailhouse.

That was enough. Gleeson stripped a blanket off the bed, climbed into his boots, shoved Corbett's note into a pocket and stealthily crossed to the door, eased it open a crack, saw nothing moving in the pitchblende hallway, stepped forth and glided along as far as Danvers' quarters. There, he pushed Corbett's note under the door so Danvers would understand, if he did not see Gleeson until sometime the following day, and went along to the downward stairway. There, though, he stopped dead-still.

A frosted night-light was burning at the clerk's desk. It shone upon a seated man reading a newspaper while sitting cross-legged in a leather chair. Some of that watery light shone against caked red-clay upon this man's boots. It also twinkled dully off this man's holstered pistol.

Gleeson turned about and started away from the lobby exit. By following out the dark hallway he came to an outside stairway—actually a fire-escape—and made his way down this to a littered back alley. Here, after a cautious reconnoitring foray which turned up no more spies, he stepped along silently as far as the rear entrance to the liverybarn. Up by the roadside doorway the nighthawk was dead to the world in a tilted-back chair, his snoring an irregularly cadenced, bubbly sound that wetly echoed, fading out and coming on.

Gleeson made his way undetected into the loft, spread his blanket upon fragrant meadow hay, and eased down there.

Out in the roadway several mounted men loped past northbound out of town. Elsewhere a little dog furiously barked in the small hours, probably disturbed by the scent of a hen-roost raider of some kind, and once several booted men walked over wood, halted and indistinguishably spoke together, then broke up heading in different directions. Gleeson smiled under his tilted-forward hat; whichever of those riders was supposed to visit Gleeson's room—if indeed any of them were—was in for a surprise.

He wiggled around to make the requisite impress, settled deeper and tried to sleep. Nothing happened; tired as he was sleep would not come. He thought of the Morgans, of their grisly reputation, of top-heavy Sheriff Riley, of Jack Corbett and of April Bannister.

He made an appointment with himself for talking to Riley's prisoner the following day. He considered the wisdom of riding out to Maple Leaf for a talk with Oliver Furth too. Not that he particularly wanted to do that; he already had a formed opinion about Furth and regardless of how he was received at Maple Leaf—after killing one Maple Leaf man and beating three others senseless, it most certainly would not be a good welcome—nothing much could come of a talk with Furth.

Better, he told himself, to leave Oliver Furth alone; better to let the cowman seek out Gleeson, or do whatever Furth thought had to be done. Then talk to him.

Downstairs the night hostler choked on a particularly damp snore, gagged and lustily coughed. Gleeson heard his chair strike down off the wall and the man's booted feet grind into dust as he rose up, went shuffling towards the harness room where there was ordinarily a cot. A rickety door squeaked open and rattled closed, all noise died out, and the barn became utterly quiet except for a horse methodically chewing somewhere below.

A troubling thought came to annoy Gleeson and prevent sleep. Who had gotten to Furth's body and had taken his pocketed pistol—and why?

He had to give that one up because as yet he did not know enough about the undercurrents of the countryside to even form a suspicion.

Corbett maybe—because of voluptuous April Bannister?

Gleeson swore at himself, yanked at the blanket, turned onto his side and closed his eyes.

FIVE

WHEN GLEESON DESCENDED from the loft, turned and violently shook his blanket to free it of chaff, a tall red-faced man stepped forth from the harness room to stop and gape.

This was Dick Banning, owner of the liverybarn, also the owner of *Banning's Bar.* From the corner of his eye Gleeson guessed the red-faced man's identity, solemnly nodded over at him, draped the blanket over his left arm and strolled forward out into the sunlighted early-morning roadway.

He was almost to the hotel when Sheriff Riley hailed him from in front of a café, turned and hurried forward. Gleeson waited.

"I been looking for you," said Riley. "Deputy U.S. lawman or not you can't just kill a man in my roadway an' walk off."

Gleeson stood there gazing down at the shorter man. "Self-defence," he said. "Ask anyone who saw it. Ask Corbett."

"Corbett didn't run out until *after* the shooting."

It began to dawn on Gleeson that the sheriff might be trying to make a case against him. He said, " 'Be pretty hard to convince a jury that when four men attacked one man—the solitary man under attack wasn't only protecting himself."

"Yeah? That cowboy's gun was still in its holster, deputy. In its holster and un-fired. How will that sound to a jury?"

Riley *was* trying to make a case, but more than that, the look in his eyes when he'd said the cowboy's gun had been in its holster, triggered another notion in Gleeson's mind. Chet Bannister was also awaiting trial because someone may have set him up like this.

Gleeson said evenly: "Why don't you hold a jury-trial and find out?"

"I've been considering it, bucko," replied Riley, his head a little to one side, his expression careful. "I could arrest you, deputy. I got the authority in my own baili-wick. U.S. lawman or not."

Gleeson's lips lifted in a cold little smile. "Why don't you try that too?" he asked, and stood there waiting for Riley to move.

"And what'd you do about it?" Riley asked, definitely cautious now.

Gleeson said, "Why Sheriff, the moment you moved I'd throw this blanket in your face with my left hand—then I'd drop you dead as a mackerel with my right hand."

Riley's gaze shifted the tiniest bit away from Gleeson's face, then firmed up again at once, but Gleeson had noticed this tell-tale sign of indecision and his faint smile broadened. He said nothing, just went on standing there in front of the hotel doorway.

Riley said: "Don't leave town," and whipped around southward, went rolling along to where a big burly man with an ivory-butted sixgun was idly leaning, gazing straight out into the roadway, then faded out back into the restaurant he'd emerged from earlier to call at Gleeson.

Several dusty horsemen jogged past out in the roadway and slyly smiled at Gleeson standing out there with that crumpled blanket over his arm. He looked at them, at his blanket, stepped on into the hotel lobby and crossed to the desk.

"Here," he said, handing the blanket to the desk-man. "It came from my upstairs room. I'll pay to have the chaff washed out of it."

The clerk looked blankly from Gleeson to the blanket and back again. He uncertainly nodded, dropped the blanket and started to face around toward the pigeon-holes behind him.

"A kid brought this letter in for you a little while ago," he said, coming back around with an envelope in his hand. "There's no name on it but he told me it was for the U.S. marshal."

Gleeson did not at once put forth his hand. It crossed his mind this might be for Bill Danvers even though his chief was incognito.

"What makes you think it's for me?" he asked.

The clerk reddened. "Well; that's the talk around town," he stammered. "I don't know, actually."

Gleeson took the envelope, walked over to that leather chair where he'd seen the cowboy with red-clay on his boots the night before, and sat down there and opened it.

Gleeson was one of those people who always looked at a signature before reading the body of a letter. This signature, though, was entirely alien to him: Mary Bonneville. He tried to recall anyone by that name, could not and read the letter. It was crisp and to the point; it said simply that if Gleeson would ride eastward from town on the stageroad at seven o'clock tonight, the writer would intercept him where it was safe and give him some information which might help prove that Chet Bannister did not murder Dean Furth.

Gleeson meticulously folded the note, pocketed it, and sat for a long time wondering who, using a woman's handwriting and the definitely feminine name of Mary Bonneville, had gone to all this trouble to get him away from Plume to bushwhack him.

He was still pondering this when he went along to the hotel dining-room, ordered a big breakfast and thoughtfully ate it, watching people come and go, mostly townsmen, watching their faces break a little with elaborate unconcern when they saw him sitting there.

Afterwards he sauntered down to the jailhouse. Riley was there rummaging through a thick sheaf of wanted flyers. He looked up when Gleeson entered, made his wicked smile and said, "Don't tell me, let me guess; you want to see Chet Bannister."

Gleeson stepped in, eased back his hat and said almost genially, "You know, Sheriff Riley, you're a lawman after my own heart; you know exactly the right thing to say at the right time—like this morning when you were screwing up your nerve to arrest me. 'Don't leave town' you said. How many men facing a shoot-out could figure a way to walk away without drawing, and still leave the impression that they'd held the whiphand all the time."

Riley, leaning over at his desk, his head crooked around, his merry little eyes unwaveringly upon Gleeson, began to very gradually redden from the throat upwards. He struck the desk hard with both palms, shoved up out of his chair and glared.

"Deputy; you got a way of callin' folks names without puttin' your tongue to 'em. I haven't forgotten what you said last night about selling out to Furth. Now—you're sayin' I'm a coward, aren't you?"

Riley had a limit. Gleeson recognized this. He was a little surprised to find it could be reached so quickly though; he had found few dishonest lawmen in his time who flared up so suddenly at being indirectly accused of perfidy. Generally they were chagrined, or else they roared with palpably false indignation. But not this one; Terry Riley was ready to fight, there was no mistaking that look or that stance. Gleeson sighed.

"You sure have a thin skin," he said. "Don't worry; I have a feeling before I leave here you and I'll have a long talk. But right now, Sheriff, all I want is to see your prisoner."

"Maybe you'd like to join him," snarled Riley. "I've got an empty cell."

Gleeson said no more; he stood on, waiting for Riley's anger to pass. When it did the sheriff snatched at a hanging ring of keys, swung around and started towards a steel-wrapped massively thick door. He fussed with the lock here briefly, flung back that sturdy panel and turned.

"Ten minutes," he snapped. "Ten minutes, deputy. If you're any longer I just might damned well close this door on the lousy pair of you."

Gleeson walked past feeling Riley's hating stare burning against him. He halted a moment for his eyes to become accustomed to the perpetual gloom of the stuffy, airless, narrowly confining, long shallow room around him. There were four steel cells side by side directly in front, across the narrow corridor where he stood peering. Only one of those cells was occupied. The man standing with his hands hooked around bars in that occupied cage was as tall as Gleeson but easily thirty pounds lighter. He was young and shockle-headed, grey-eyed and bitter-faced.

"You Bannister?" asked Gleeson, stepping closer.

"Yeah; who're you; a new Maple Leaf hand?"

Gleeson palmed his badge where Bannister could see it. The cowboy's eyes widened, a little of that settled bleakness lifted from around his lips, his eyes. He drew closer to the bars. "You find the gun?" he quickly asked. Then he said, dropping his voice, "Get me out of here, Marshal. Riley's in with 'em. They figure to lynch me."

"Is that so," said Gleeson mildly. "How do you know that?"

"Dewey Porter slipped up to the outside window last night and told me."

Gleeson rummaged for a face to fit the name Dewey Porter, found none, then remembered reading that Porter

43

was Oliver Furth's ranch foreman. The name had been in Corbett's note.

"You and Dewey friendly?" Gleeson asked the youth.

Bannister's face twisted. "Friendly hell; he slipped up to tell me that so's I'd sweat."

"Looks like he succeeded," Gleeson commented dryly. "For now forget Porter. Tell me—did you see Furth's gun?"

"See it? Hell no. Nobody ever saw Dean's gun. But I sure-enough saw the bulge of it when he stuck his hand in his pocket."

"All right," said Gleeson. "Now tell me—who is Mary Bonneville?" He watched young Bannister closely on this one, but there was no surprise, no hesitation at all.

"She was Dewey's girl until April came along. Why; what about her?"

"Nothing for now. Give me one more answer and I'll let you go back to counting the bars. Who besides you would want Dean Furth dead?"

"Besides me? Dammit deputy, I had nothing particular against Dean. Not until he started making a play for my wife."

"All right, all right. Calm down and answer my question: Who else wanted him dead?"

Bannister's brows rolled downward. "He was a bully. He had his paw's money behind him. He had the best horses, the best saddles. He had a tough crew of riders behind him. He made trouble anywhere he felt like it and folks sidestepped a showdown with him because of who he was. Hell; ask half the rangemen for thirty miles in any direction. They'll tell you Dean didn't have a single

44

friend unless it was ones his paw's money bought for him. Even some of the Maple Leaf riders hated his guts. He was a bully and he always wore hide-out guns so's he'd have the edge if anyone tried anything rough with him. You know; he never looked armed so the cowboys were never sure whether they'd ought to draw on him or not—that's how he got the drop on 'em. He didn't have the guts to make a stand-up fight. Ask Jack Corbett; Dean roughed up at least a dozen fellers in Jack's place an' got away with it every time because the other fellers either feared his old man's money and power, or they didn't think he was armed."

"Sounds like a real lovable feller," muttered Gleeson. "Thanks, Bannister. I'll probably see you again. By the way, in case Riley hasn't gotten around to telling you, Corbett's put your wife to work so she won't starve, although he doesn't seem to have many customers left since the Furth killing. I don't know yet whether you deserve a friend like that or whether you don't, but I'll tell you this much from experience; damned few men in the bad trouble you're in, have 'em."

"Deputy, wait! Listen; get me out of here. Dewey Porter wasn't just tryin' to scare me with that lynch talk."

Gleeson went over to the door, stopped and turned. "If Porter comes back, Bannister, you tell him for me he's got to have more luck than a saint to bust you out of here, but if he thinks he can do it, to go right ahead and try."

Gleeson passed on out of the cell-block, caught Sheriff Riley's steady eye as he emerged, turned, swung the cell-block door closed, snapped the lock and paced doorward past Riley's desk and Riley's hooded, unsmiling eyes.

Outside again, Gleeson walked as far as Jack Corbett's place. Here, he again found Corbett and April Bannister alone. April was wiping table-tops and Corbett was polishing glasses behind his bar. He looked around, saw who his customer was and drew a glass of ale, gravely set it before Gleeson and gave the edges of his big moustache a hard twist.

"I don't make any money this way," Corbett said, nodding at the ale, "but at least I keep on the right side of the law." He made a wry smile.

Gleeson lifted the glass, saluted Corbett with it and drank deeply, set it down and put his palm over it to indicate he wished no re-fill. "Thanks for the warning last night."

"Did you take it?"

"Yeah; I holed up in the liverybarn loft."

"And tonight?" said Corbett.

"I never worry about tonight until it gets here, Corbett. Tell me something; were there any Maple Leaf men in here the evening Bannister shot Furth?"

Corbett had no chance to answer. From half way across the quiet room April Bannister looked up and said, "Yes; at least five that I recognized. You didn't think Dean would try anything without his crew, did you, deputy?"

"Thanks," said Gleeson, turned and walked out of the saloon.

SIX

EVENING CAME SLOWLY for Phil Gleeson. He lay sprawled on his bed at the hotel alternately drowsing and thinking. There was a Mary Bonneville after all, and if she'd been Dewey Porter's girl and had been jilted in favour of April Bannister, then that set some kind of a record for the Maple Leaf. One man had already died because of April—Dean Furth. Another was in jail charged with murder—Chet Bannister. Now Maple Leaf's rangeboss Dewey Porter had his eye on April.

Gleeson arose, washed his face in cold water to clear away the last of his late-day drowsiness, and made a little clucking sound. April had what the cowboys liked, he would never deny that, but in his own rutting days, thought Gleeson, a girl with that much sultriness in her gaze and that much violence in her immediate past, never would have attracted him.

He left the hotel with evening coming down from the far-away mountains in a broad, soft shading of pearly grey. By the time he'd gotten astride, over at Banning's barn, dusk was well settled in upon the land. He left town riding leisurely northward; he kept right on going in the wrong direction until he could barely make Plume out down the back-trail, which meant anyone watching back there could no longer see him either, then he cut around southeasterly and loped for an hour, or until he saw the faint luminosity of the wind-cleansed stageroad. He turned eastward here, rode for another hour, then left the road, went along paralleling it until he was confident he must be nearing the point of rendezvous, and he halted, got down, yanked forth his Winchester saddle-gun and walked ahead of his horse where he could not be readily skylined by an ambusher, but where he conversely could skyline anyone roundabout who might be sitting upon a horse.

A man playing a rough game observes rough rules. Gleeson sighted the rider—or rather his horse did and alerted Gleeson by momentarily hanging back—after about a mile of walking through short, wiry forage grass.

It was a woman too. Gleeson dropped down, remained like a stone until the horse fidgeted a little, tired of standing, and Gleeson caught the unmistakable high swelling of a woman's profiled upper body. He did not go forward even then, though. He left his horse, made a big circle looking for others in the soft-lighted moonless night, then glided in behind the woman, stopped, raised his carbine and deliberately cocked it.

That little sound had a way of chilling people to the marrow, particularly from behind. "Get down," he ordered quietly. "Keep both your hands in plain sight and turn around."

The woman obeyed stiffly. She was tall for a woman, long-legged and tiny waisted and startlingly handsome. She wore no gun at her waist and no booted carbine under the fender of her rigged-out horse. Gleeson lowered the carbine, eased off the hammer, relaxed to stand hipshot, and went close enough for a good look at this surprisingly handsome woman.

He recognized her at once; it was the same woman

who had ridden the coach into Plume the night before with Bill Danvers, She had blue-black hair, almond-shaped dark eyes, and a full, wilful mouth heavy at the centre, and a direct, almost challenging way of returning a man's stare, almost as though she were offering a challenge, daring a man to break the composure of her face, daring him to prove she was wrong in her obvious scorn of men.

"I'm Gleeson," he said, finally. "I got your note at the hotel. You're Mary Bonneville—Dewey Porter's ex-girlfriend."

"Hardly that," said Mary Bonneville shortly. "Dewey wanted it that way but we had a difference of opinion."

Gleeson shrugged. "Have it any way you want it, lady," he said briskly. "I don't even know the man, and from what I've heard I'm not sure I want to. About that note. . . ."

Mary Bonneville stepped up, reached inside the lower portion of her bodice, drew forth a Colt Lightning pistol and held it toward Gleeson. He looked at that pointing barrel, at Mary Bonneville's expressionless face, and wavered between two simultaneous thoughts.

"Take it," she said, pushing the little gun at him. "You want the gun that was taken from Dean Furth's coat pocket the night he was killed, don't you?"

Gleeson still stood there looking from those blank, almost scornful dark eyes, to that pistol. He made no move to reach out. "How would I ever prove that was Furth's gun?"

"By checking the serial number with the man who sold it to him three years ago in Cheyenne."

49

Gleeson finally took the gun. He flipped open the gate, spun the cylinder, saw pale starshine twinkle off six loaded chambers, closed the gate and pushed the weapon into his waistband.

"And who might the man be who sold this thing, ma'am?"

"William Bonneville, the Cheyenne gunsmith."

Gleeson drew in a breath, let it softly out, and continued to study that beautiful, cold and scornful face across from him in the increasing dark. "This William Bonneville—he'd be your husband; right?"

"Wrong, deputy. He'd be my brother."

"And he gave you this gun?"

Mary shook her head. "I sent it to him for identification after Bannister killed Furth. He sent it back with a note verifying it as the same gun he'd sold Dean three years before."

"Another question, ma'am: How did you come by this gun?"

"I was there at Corbett's place the evening Dean was killed. In fact, before April Bannister walked in, Dean and I were having a drink at his table. Afterwards, when Dean fell down, I was the second person to kneel beside him."

"Let me interrupt a minute," said Gleeson quickly. "Who was the first person?"

"I'm coming to that, deputy," said this tall, cold girl, then paused to consider Gleeson tartly. "As I said, when Dean went down, I ran over and knelt beside him. He still had his hand in his coat pocket. The man who had gotten there ahead of me—the first person to Dean's side, was removing his hand. He also removed something else—that gun you have now—and it was cocked to fire."

Gleeson leaned upon his carbine. He was eloquently silent. This was the key to the riddle. He'd never before received such a key, though, from so desirable a witness.

Mary Bonneville returned his regard with that same unflinching, cold look, as though she saw in Phil Gleeson a man like all other men. Then he spoke and the duel was ended.

"Dewey Porter?"

She nodded. "The first person to reach Dean was Dewey Porter; you are correct. For a man who claims never to have met Dewey you've made an excellent judgement of him, deputy."

Gleeson let this pass. "Since that night, ma'am, where have you been?"

Mary put her head a little to one side looking sceptical now. "I see you haven't gotten all the answers though."

"Lady; I just arrived in Plume yesterday afternoon."

Mary's handsome lips faintly lifted at their outer corners at this strained protest from Gleeson. "I apologize, deputy. I've been out at my ranch. But if you haven't heard about me you wouldn't know about my ranch, would you? It's four miles east of town and a little southward. I live there alone, except for two old cowboys, left-overs from my father's time when we ran cattle."

"I see. Right after the Furth shooting you skedaddled; is that right?"

Mary inclined her head. "Dean was his father's only child. Oliver Furth is a very bad man to have against

51

you. I didn't want him to think I was implicated in any way with what happened. Also, I wanted to go to Cheyenne and ask my brother about that gun. That's where I went."

Gleeson reached up, scratched the tip of his nose and critically eyed Mary Bonneville. "You were at the table with Dean. The saloon was crowded that night according to Jack Corbett. You were seen by Dewey Porter, other Maple Leaf men, and probably fifty others who probably recognized you—yet you now say you—"

"I can see now," Mary interrupted to coldly say, "that being a deputy U.S. marshal doesn't make you infallible in your deductions, Mister Gleeson. I said I didn't want Oliver Furth to think I had anything to do with his son's killing. I mean by that at one time Oliver wanted me to marry Dean. I refused. I didn't want him to think there was anything new between us."

"Like maybe—?"

"Put any interpretation upon it you wish," said Mary sharply, beginning to turn away. "You have the gun."

"Wait a minute, ma'm. The gun's not worth a plugged nickel without your sworn statement that you saw Dewey Porter take it out of Furth's pocket, cocked and ready to fire at Bannister."

Mary halted, swung back and faced Gleeson with her distant look. "If I'd dared give you that, Mister Gleeson, I wouldn't have had to secretly meet you in the night. Oliver Furth wants Chet Bannister prosecuted for his son's death. He's getting the countryside up against Bannister. How long do you think I'd be alive if I turned up as the only witness against Dean, his father, and Dewey

Porter?" Mary raised one sturdy, tanned hand. "This long," she said, holding her first and second fingers an inch apart, "and not one second longer."

Gleeson let her walk back to her horse before lifting his carbine and hiking over to stand at the animal's shoulder. "Strange thing about people," he drawled. "They want justice done; they just never have the guts to do it themselves."

Mary swiftly raised her reins. Gleeson reached out, caught them below the horse's chin and powerfully held them. "Thanks for the gun though," he said up into her face. "It was worth the ride out here. So was something else, ma'm: The vision of as lovely a woman as I've ever seen in my whole life—with the soul of a mouse." He released the reins, pushed the horse off and smartly slapped its rump. Mary Bonneville was lost to his sight in less than a minute.

Gleeson returned where he'd left his own horse, made a cigarette, lit it behind his hat, swung up over leather and headed back towards Plume. As he rode along slouched and thoughtful, smoke drifting upwards to make him squint, he closely and carefully examined the Lightning model Colt pistol with its fully loaded six chambers Mary Bonneville had given him. He also examined the image still in his head of that cold, flawless face, that perfect figure, and that coldly disdaining look in those midnight-coloured large liquid eyes.

It was a pleasant warm night with the scent of a sighing earth yielding up its stored heat from the day's bright, hot sun. Overhead burned ten thousand distant campfires of departed warriors, as the old Indian belief said, and across the vaulted heavens rode the flaming tail-races made by great chieftains heading home from raids.

Gleeson passed along through all this thinking his sombre thoughts. He had forgotten Jack Corbett's warning. He had temporarily forgotten too, Bill Danvers and Danvers' reason for being in Plume.

He came down out of the velvet east bearing toward the lodestar-lights dead ahead where Plume lay distance-shrouded, entirely lost in his private world, when out of the black north he heard three horsemen loping along towards the same orange lights towards which he was also riding, their steady, muted hooffalls sounding solid and close-spaced.

Perhaps, he thought, they would be Maple Leaf riders. Perhaps riders from one of the other cow outfits north and possibly east of town. He halted, dropped both hands to his saddlehorn and traced out the unseen passage of those men by their sounds. When they were past, he resumed his onward way content that now no chance existed of encountering those three.

Distantly, out back of town somewhere, a stud-horse whistled its trumpeting call. Distantly too a dog bayed. Beyond that there was nothing to hear; even those three riders had gone beyond Gleeson's range of hearing.

He got as close to town as he wished to get, swung westerly and began riding in a big circle around Plume. Where he located a fenced-in graveyard atop a gentle roll of land, he dismounted, off-saddled, hobbled his horse, spread his blanket against a backdrop of headstones and askew wooden crosses, tossed away his hat and lay down.

It was, he told himself, a singular thing that after anticipating a real bed for so long, and after paying for one at the hotel in town, he was now taking his rest upon the ground again.

He scarcely considered his hushed surroundings at all; to a man who knew death as intimately as any living person can know it, cemeteries held no fear. In fact, if Corbett's warning of the night before still held true and an attempt might be made on his life, it was very unlikely an assassin would think of looking for his victim in a graveyard—*before* he killed him.

Gleeson watched those infrequent flaming meteors. He listened to the singing stillness around him. He thought that whether he liked it or not, on the morrow he was going to have to hunt up Oliver Furth and Dewey Porter for a talk.

With that resolution stowed away, he closed his eyes and instantly fell asleep.

SEVEN

THERE WERE TWO WAYS to approach the Maple Leaf ranch. One, the most commonly used entrance and the simplest, was directly overland by wagon-road from the north-south roadway. This was not the way Gleeson went there; he followed the crooked cattle trails which meandered across Maple Leaf range for an hour before swinging up and over a westerly rib of rolling land, and downward into the grassy meadow where a little creek ran, where silvery cottonwoods stood shading summer-hardened earth, and where a casual sprawl of dark buildings stood.

He studied Maple Leaf's headquarters from that slight eminence, eased his horse out and rode down across the meadow into the yard with the sun just beginning to brighten an easterly sky.

He tied up before the main house, ducked under the hitchrack, halted when a sixth-sense told him to and half swung to face across the empty yard.

There was a large bunkhouse across the way, south of a monstrous log barn and north of a shoeing-shed. Two men were standing upon the bunkhouse porch over there like carved statues. Both were staring over where Gleeson was as though astonished to find him here. Another man came easing out around those two; he also looked and abruptly halted. A fourth and fifth man also pushed out. These last two had just arisen; one was holding boots in his hand while the other was vigorously scratching a tousled head.

Gleeson waited for one of those men to call, to step out toward him, to make some hostile move but none of them did. He was sure at least three of those cowboys knew him, had violently encountered him before, but because it had been dark the night he'd exploded into a brawl with them, he could not determine one from the other.

Gleeson turned his back, crossed to the main house front door and rolled fisted knuckles over wood making an echoing reverberation bounce around inside, striking from wall to wall.

The wait was not long. When a man appeared he was

a little annoyed looking, clearly he'd expected someone other than the rough-looking stranger facing him. This man was perhaps fifty years old; he was grey over the temples with a hard grey set of level eyes. His nose had a high-bridged, hawkish look. His mouth was a wide, bloodless slit across the lower section of his sun-blasted face and he was compactly put together, strong and muscular.

"Oliver Furth?" asked Gleeson, pushing a hand into a pocket and letting it lie there. The man nodded, shadings of a dawning suspicion firming up in his glance. Gleeson withdrew the hand with his palmed badge in it. Furth looked, seemed not the least surprised, but when he raised his eyes to Gleeson's face again, they were like wet granite.

"What do you want?" Furth asked.

"A few answers," said Gleeson. "First off—why don't you let the courts handle what you think is a murder?"

Furth's jaw snapped closed. His eyes flamed and a vein at the side of his head swelled ominously. He struggled for a moment, then he said in a voice as quiet, as menacing as distant gunfire, "I have no faith in your law courts, deputy. An eye for an eye is good enough for me."

"Even if it wasn't murder?"

"It *was* murder!"

Gleeson stood there gazing at Furth, coming to a hard decision: This man was beyond reasoning with. Gleeson had met this type before; they would destroy anyone, anything, that got between them and what they held to be right and proper. He reached into his belt, drew forth the little gun Mary Bonneville had given him, and showed it to Furth. "This was your son's, Mister Furth. It was taken off him the night of the killing."

Those icy eyes dropped, stared in a fascinated way at the pistol and remained there as Gleeson went on speaking.

"I know who removed that gun. What I want to know now—is why?"

Furth tore his glance away and raised it. "That's not true, deputy. After the killing I made it a point to seek out everyone who was there, that night. Not a one of them saw a gun. Not a one of them."

"Two of them did, Mister Furth, and I've done a little asking around myself." Gleeson twisted, looked out across the yard, saw that the Maple Leaf riders were standing elaborately idle over by the bunkhouse facing forward, every one of them armed and sober-faced, and said, "Which one of those men is Dewey Porter?"

"Why?" demanded Oliver Furth, for the first time since this meeting began, moving, stepping forward out of the doorway onto the porch.

"I'd like you to hear him answer a couple of questions."

Furth looked over, called out Porter's name, and stood waiting with Gleeson as an easy-moving tall man cut away from those others and started houseward.

Gleeson studied this one closely. Dewey Porter was as solid, as lithe and deceptively slow-looking as Gleeson himself was. He was dark and swarthy and possessed of an aura of violence that preceded him to the porch. When he halted just off the veranda he ran a slow, assessing glance up and down Phil Gleeson.

"Dewey," said Furth. "This is a deputy U.S. lawman. You see that Lightning model Colt he's holding; he says someone took that off Dean's body the night Bannister killed Dean."

Porter glanced at the gun without any expression showing. He glanced up into Gleeson's eyes then on over to Furth. He showed nothing at all; no surprise, no apprehension, no belief or disbelief. Gleeson told himself this Dewey Porter was a cool one, a dangerous one.

"It probably looks like Dean's gun, Mister Furth, but I was the first one to get to him after the murder. There was no gun on him. That I know for a fact."

Gleeson thoughtfully pushed the Colt Lightning back into his trouser-band. He knew as confidently as he knew anything, Porter was lying. He also knew he could not prove that this was so, and it angered him.

He said: "Porter; why exactly did your four men jump me in town night before last?"

Porter looked blandly at Gleeson. He shrugged. "Ask them, deputy. They might know but I sure don't." He paused, his eyes turned unwaveringly cold. "If I was to guess though, I'd say it was because you got your nose where it don't belong. We got law in Plume. We handle our own troubles without outside interference. It could be that folks're beginnin' to resent you, deputy. Not just Maple Leaf riders but a lot of other folks as well."

That, Gleeson knew, was a warning to him; a threat against him. He looked back at Porter giving stare for stare. "And you," he asked softly. "How do you feel about the federal law, Porter?"

Furth's rangeboss spread his hands, he changed expression. "You got a job to do," he said easily, almost slyly. "Go ahead and do it. I reckon you fellers get paid for your busted skulls and graveside rites. It's all the same to me—except that I figure you're sure tryin' hard to make something here that isn't going to jell for you. Dean was murdered, deputy, an' I know that for a fact."

Gleeson, thinking this swarthy, bland and thoroughly treacherous man was probably the reason behind Furth and Bannister fighting, nodded his head up and down. "You might be right at that," he murmured. Oliver Furth's head jerked; he stared at Gleeson obviously accepting this as it had sounded to him; as though Gleeson was beginning to believe his son's killing had been murder. But not Dewey Porter; he caught the innuendo and kept staring at Gleeson from an expressionless face.

Something passed between these two; some tough knowledge of inherent enmity. It was as though they both understood what the real truth was, and understood also that the other one knew this.

Porter looked over at Oliver Furth, almost disdainfully dismissing Gleeson. "If there's nothing else," he calmly said, "maybe I'd better line the boys out for the day's work."

Furth nodded. "Yes, you'd better do that," he agreed. "And thanks, Dewey."

Porter ignored Gleeson to say softly, "Any time, Oliver. Any time at all." He put his broad back to Gleeson and went hiking back over the yard toward those waiting, silent riders.

"Anything else?" Furth asked, his tone turning brisk again, his eyes cutting around to Gleeson as hard and uncompromising as ever.

"One more thing, Mister Furth. If I told you I could prove this gun was your son's and he was carrying it the night he was shot—what would you say?"

"Deputy, I'd say you were deliberately trying to protect a murderer, and I'd tell you exactly what Dewey just told you—get your nose out of where it doesn't belong!"

Furth swung back towards his house. Gleeson's control slipped a little; he reached out, caught Furth's arm and roughly spun him back around.

"Furth, I think you've made some bad mistakes in your lifetime, but none as big as the mistake you're making now. Listen to me; you keep on the way you're going and you'll think the sky fell on you. I can understand a man grieving for his only son. What I can't understand is compounding a killing by causing other killings. Take my advice, Furth; call it off before it's too late."

The cowman's face turned white. His eyes flamed with wrath made worse because he did not speak. He stood like that briefly, then whipped around, passed over into his house and violently slammed the door.

Gleeson stood there turning limp, turning dispirited. He swung his head, saw those waiting men watching him coldly on across the yard, went down to his horse, untied, swung up and reined around to slowly pass on across the Maple Leaf yard riding southward back towards town.

All the way back it bothered him that he could find no

solid reason for Porter deliberately framing the killing of Dean Furth, unless it was over some secret hunger he felt for Bannister's wife. He thought he'd talk to April when he got back.

That was the only reason he could come up with for what Porter had obviously done, and yet it seemed weak. Why involve his boss's son? If he'd wanted Bannister out of the way, why hadn't he simply trumped up his own trouble with Bannister?

Gleeson was just short of Plume, about a half mile out, when he remembered what he'd heard about Dean Furth. Even his own men, Bannister had told him, despised Furth's son. Had he meant Dewey Porter too?

It was entirely possible. Obviously Porter had been a Maple Leaf rider for a long time; long enough to come to know his boss's son and hate his guts if Dean had been the kind of a bully it seemed that he had in fact been.

One thing Gleeson had not mentioned back at the Maple Leaf; the dried red-clay he'd noticed on Porter's boots. The same kind of red-clay that had been on the boots of that waiting man he'd spied in the hotel lobby the night Corbett had warned him he might be assassinated in his bed.

All right, he told himself, Porter is in this up to his ears, and for lack of anything else to rely upon, it would be safe to assume Porter hated Dean Furth. He had then somehow egged him into a fight with Chet Bannister. If he wanted Dean dead he'd gotten his wish. If he'd also wanted Bannister out of the way so he could have an open field with Bannister's voluptuous wife, he'd also succeeded there. But what stuck in Gleeson's craw was how Porter had also drawn the dead man's anguished father into the thing so deftly that Oliver Furth was on the way to destroying himself in his misplaced compulsion for vengeance.

Two mounted men appeared side by side out of a little draw east of Gleeson. He saw them and yanked back at the same time, his gun hand whipping downward, his brain clearing instantly and freshening to new peril.

One of those men curved thin lips in a slow, cold smile. He said across the little separating distance, "Phil; you're getting slow or old or too wrapped up in your thoughts. Hell; we could have shot the buttons off your shirt before you even knew we were around."

That one was Charley Barrett, the deputy marshal Danvers had sent for. The other one with Charley was short, massive, seasoned Bert McKay. Gleeson let his breath out with a pungent curse. He couldn't think of anything appropriate to say so he said nothing. The two men rode up and halted.

"Where's Danvers?" McKay asked.

"In town," answered Gleeson, then swore at those two again. They smiled at him. "I ought to rub your lousy noses in the dirt," he growled. "Slippin' up on me like that."

Charley, a sleepy-acting freckled man, said, "We didn't know it was you until you came slouchin' along right past us."

"Who the hell were you expecting; Danvers?"

Bert shook his head, still smiling but not with his eyes. "Not Danvers, Phil. We thought it might be Moe or Cal or Ralph Morgan."

Gleeson's face smoothed out. He glanced from one of those near-grinning faces to the other one. "Are they here?"

"Rode in sometime last night," said Barrett. "We were pushin' along behind 'em."

Gleeson remembered hearing three horsemen passing by in the darkness when he was returning from his meeting with Mary Bonneville. "I'll be damned," he murmured.

"You will be if you run into them wearin' your badge," agreed McKay cheerfully. "They haven't had their lawman for breakfast since the killing of Constable Fellers down near Dodge City."

EIGHT

GLEESON LEFT MCKAY AND BARRETT, rode alone into Plume, put up his horse and crossed to Jack Corbett's saloon. Corbett was there but Gleeson wasn't looking for him.

He went up to the bar, leaned upon it and said "Where's April?"

Corbett jerked a hand over his shoulder indicating the quarters beyond his bar. "In her room. Why?"

"I need a couple of answers," said Gleeson. "To start with—just how good with a gun was Chet Bannister?"

Corbett made a slow and knowing smile. "You're beginnin' to ask the right questions, deputy, you must be on the right trail."

"What does that mean, Corbett?"

"Well; I couldn't plant the ideas in your head; you'd

64

have rejected them. That's the way folks are." Corbett put a speculative look upon Gleeson, smiled and said. "You're wondering why someone had Dean Furth sitting there when Bannister was also in the barroom. You're wondering how April happened in an' how come Dean to make his play for her." Corbett stopped again. This time he brought up the inevitable two glasses of ale, handed Gleeson one and kept one for himself.

"I'll tell you, deputy. Chet Bannister is one of the fastest men with a gun you ever saw. But he wasn't a troublesome feller, an' when you couple these two things you ordinarily get a man other men pretty much like and don't pick fights with."

"That's not the way I heard it from Riley."

"Of course not. You didn't expect Riley to say anything good about Bannister, did you?"

Gleeson sipped his ale without replying.

"Deputy, listen a minute. About a year back Bannister tangled with Dewey Porter right where you're standing. It was over a card game. Dewey went for his gun. He didn't even get it clear of his holster when Chet had him starin' into a pistol barrel. Now let me ask you; would you, if you wanted a man like that out of the way, try and shoot it out with him when you knew you didn't have the chance of a snowball in hell?"

Gleeson slowly shook his head. Corbett had just answered one of the riddles in his head.

"Now let's suppose you wanted a girl belongin' to this same man who could out-draw an' out-shoot you—"

"I get the picture you're painting, Corbett. Why didn't you tell me these things yesterday?"

"Like I said a minute ago, deputy. I couldn't plant these ideas in your head then; you just didn't know enough about these people or about what happened. You'd have avoided me as some kind of vengeful man with a bad grudge against Porter."

Gleeson put down his glass, drew forth the Lightning model Colt and placed it upon the bartop. Corbett's reaction was instantaneous. He stared, dropped a muttered swear word and began to bitterly smile and twist his fierce moustache.

"Where did you get it?"

Gleeson shrugged, turning aside this query with his silence. "It was Furth's. I'm satisfied about that. Now tell me—if Dewey Porter removed this gun from Furth's body a couple of seconds after he was downed by Bannister, why would he do it; I mean, aside from wanting Bannister out of the way so he could get at April, why didn't he just hire some two-bit back-shooter to kill Bannister; why involve his boss's son?"

"That's an easy one," answered Corbett without any hesitation. "He wants Maple Leaf."

"The ranch? You mean he got Oliver's boy killed thinking he'd get the ranch?"

Corbett nodded. "And he will too."

"How; he's only the rangeboss?"

Corbett looked wry. "He happens to also be the only son of Oliver Furth's dead sister, deputy."

Gleeson looked into his empty glass a moment, until his surprise passed, then he pushed the glass aside, leaned over the bar and said, "Corbett; you have interesting customers."

"Had," said Jack Corbett with a sardonic expression. "Had, deputy, not have. I might as well close up. There's hardly been a man in here since you showed up."

"There will be, Corbett." Gleeson straightened back and solemnly winked. "I wouldn't be surprised if all of a sudden you started getting a new customer or two." He fished for his tobacco sack, went to work manufacturing a cigarette, and said without looking up, "Who was at Furth's table with him the night he got his deep six?"

"Mary Bonneville. She was already in here when Dean and Dewey and the other Maple Leafers arrived. Dean sat down with her, started his laughin' and teasin'."

"Tell me about her," said Gleeson, lighting up, exhaling, and with his eyes steadily upon Jack Corbett.

"Well; she's pretty handsome, deputy. Most of the boys hereabouts at one time or another have made a play for her, including Dean and Dewey and ten dozen more."

"She's got a ranch out of town, hasn't she?"

Corbett's eyes drew out narrow. He considered Gleeson carefully for a moment before he said, "Listen; with me you don't have to play any games. You're interested in Mary—just say so."

"All right; I'm interested."

"That's better. Mary's maybe twenty-five, twenty-six; she's disillusioned where men are concerned. Her trouble is she can see through fellers like Dean and Dewey at one glance. That's kept her from gettin' married, I expect."

"How about her truthfulness?"

Corbett made an emphatic gesture. "Solid as rock," he

pronounced. "Mary Bonneville's word is better than two-thirds of the promises of the best men in this damned country, deputy."

Gleeson smoked on, carefully piecing his puzzle together. It was almost completed now. He let a little smile shadow his lips. Not bad; in two days—not two full days yet—he'd gotten to the source of the trouble in Plume. He was congratulating himself when Corbett said something that crumpled his self-esteem in a twinkling.

"Now you know the why and the wherefores. What I'm wondering about, deputy, is what you're going to do about them. You see, this morning early when I was walkin' up the back-alley to open the saloon, I saw Terry Riley talkin' to three damned rough looking men behind the general store down a few doors. One of those men put up his hands, encircled his own gullet like he was simulating a hanging, and said so's I heard it: 'If you're sure they're ready to go, go ahead and buy 'em the whisky tonight. We'll be around watching; when everything's ready you just fade out an' leave the rest to us'."

Gleeson's cigarette died between his lips. He and Jack Corbett exchanged a long look. Gleeson slowly reached up, removed the cigarette and dropped it on the floor. He had no doubt at all who those three men had been.

"Tonight, eh?" he said.

Corbett nodded, watching the deputy U.S. marshal and remaining totally quiet.

"Well," sighed Gleeson, "I guess I miss sleepin' in that bed I paid for one more night." He turned and left the saloon, swung southward as far as the hotel, hiked across the lobby and went heavily up the stairs.

For some reason he could not define exactly, Gleeson had an uneasy premonition. He fished for the key to his room, found it, bent to insert it, and the locked door opened silently inward under his hand. He moved only his eyes.

Bill Danvers was standing there gazing at Gleeson from a blank face. He stepped back, motioned, and carefully closed the door when Gleeson was inside.

McKay and Barrett were sprawled over by the roadside window. They had evidently been watching the roadway, but now they were looking up from their chairs at Phil Gleeson.

From behind him Danvers said, "Phil; this hick-town sheriff is in it with the Morgans up to his Irish ears."

Gleeson tossed his hat upon a dresser, ran crooked fingers through his hair, felt his beard-stubble and sarcastically said, "You don't tell me." He went to the water pitcher, filled a basin, turned under his shirt collar and prepared to wash and shave. As a sort of afterthought he pulled out Dean Furth's pistol and tossed it carelessly over onto the bed.

"That was the gun taken off Furth the night he was shot. It's loaded and I've got it on good authority that he had cocked it in his pocket before he got out-gunned and killed. As for Riley—I don't know his reasons, but I've known since yesterday he was hand-in-glove with Dewey Porter and Oliver Furth."

The three other men remained motionless watching Gleeson whip up a lather, apply it, and begin to carefully shave himself with a wicked looking bone-handled straight-razor.

"I'll tell you something else too," he muttered between razor strokes. "The Morgans met Riley in an alley this morning and laid all the groundwork for bad trouble tonight. Riley's to stand the drinks, get everyone fired up, then step out and let the Morgans take over."

Danvers absorbed this with a gathering scowl. "A lynching?" he asked.

Gleeson finished shaving, examined himself carefully, splashed in the water basin and turned about as he began drying off. "What else?" he asked, and tossed the towel aside. "If Furth hired the Morgans; what else?"

"It isn't like them though," growled sleepy-eyed Charley Barrett. "We've practically camped in their shadows for a year, Phil. They aren't devious men." He looked over at burly, short Bert McKay as though for confirmation of this. "If Furth wants this Bannister killed an' if he's got the local law in the palm of his hand, the way the Morgans would earn their money would be to simply walk down there, step into Riley's jailhouse, find this Bannister in the cell and shoot him to death. As simple as that."

Gleeson was turning his collar right-side-out as he listened. Now he said, "You're overlooking something, Charley. It's Oliver Furth's money and it's Oliver Furth giving the orders. He doesn't want the town against him, he wants it implicated along with him."

Danvers' scowl smoothed out at this. He nodded. "I think Phil's right."

Bert McKay yawned, hid this behind a ham-like paw, and pushed up out of his chair. "Knowin' how it's to

70

happen is half the battle," he said, scooping up a battered old hat and carelessly dragging it over his head. "How about it, Bill; do we do the obvious?"

Danvers strolled to the window, clasped both hands behind him and stared out. The others watched him, patiently waiting. Gleeson crossed to his bed, sat down on the side of it, put a hand behind him and tested the mattress with a rueful expression.

Danvers turned. "Yeah, we do the obvious. But the obvious in this case is get inside the jailhouse and wait there."

"And this sheriff; what about him?" asked Barrett.

Danvers shrugged. "If he makes trouble we either lock him up, hit him over the head, or whatever's got to be done. I tell you frankly boys, I'm not nearly as interested in Riley or Furth or this Bannister as I am in nailing the damned Morgan brothers once and for all."

Gleeson looked wryly upwards. Danvers caught that expression. His face softened a little. "I don't mean to belittle your job here," he said to Phil. "But you've got to admit the Morgans are a lot more important than this other thing."

Gleeson's expression didn't change. "I never have figured the life of an outlaw, or three outlaws, equalled the life of an honest man, Bill."

Danvers looked exasperated. "All right, Phil, all right. We'll be in there protecting your man—this Bannister. All I'm saying is, if there's trouble, our primary concern should be to get those damned Morgans."

"Amen," murmured Charley Barrett. Standing in the centre of the room Bert McKay solemnly nodded assent to this.

Danvers went on speaking, his words turning crisp, his delivery of them hard. "We'll drift down to the jailhouse one at a time. I'll go first. The rest of you keep watch along the sidewalk. When I head out, time yourselves; let maybe fifteen minutes pass, then each of you stroll down and come in too. If Riley's in there. . . ." Danvers raised big shoulders and let them fall. "That'll be up to him. If he wants trouble he'll get a gut-full. If he doesn't, we'll just lock him up. After that we wait."

Gleeson looked doubtful. "It's likely to be a pretty big crowd of 'em, Bill, all drunk or half-drunk, all armed and loaded for bear."

Danvers nodded at this. "And that jailhouse looks mighty stout to me," he said. "Besides, it's too late to do anything else."

"We maybe could slip Bannister out of town, Bill."

"Not a damned chance, Phil. I don't think we could have successfully done that even yesterday. Too many men watching; too many men kept posted about everything by Riley. Anyway, as I told you before, if we need bait to get a crack at the Morgans, we'll use Bannister."

The others put their steady eyes over upon Gleeson. He saw this, understood what McKay and Barrett were wondering, and afterwards said no more; simply sat there listening to U.S. Marshal Big Bill Danvers work it all out tentatively in crisp, short sentences.

"If there's shooting, boys, get those damned Morgans first. Concentrate on 'em no matter what. As for the stupid townsmen and cowboys—try only to wing 'em."

Gleeson was thinking of what Jack Corbett had said; if

the federal law hadn't come all this lynch-talk would have died down because not enough people could be influenced by Oliver Furth. He wondered about that.

NINE

RILEY WOULD HAVE TOLD the Morgans there was a federal lawman in town. Gleeson was confident of that. He was also confident that by now Riley had sent word to the Maple Leaf, to Porter and perhaps Furth, that this was to be the night for Chet Bannister to die.

Still, when he left his room at the hotel and stepped out onto the sidewalk, Plume was as outwardly as unconcerned and otherwise busy as always. It was difficult, standing there idly gazing over the place, to believe this thriving little town was a powder-keg.

Barrett and McKay drifted out separately, looking like run-of-the-mill cowhands, drifters with a little roundup pay still tinkling in their pockets. Bill Danvers was different; when he passed Gleeson sedately walking along looking neither right nor left, he appeared to be exactly what he'd given the impression that he was; a successful cowman.

Phil stood in late afternoon shade making a smoke he did not want; using this little time-consuming chore as a screen to hide his sharp study of Plume, the people he saw scattered throughout town, and the atmosphere, the mood of the place. When he lit up, tossed away his broken match, he could find nothing at all suspicious, so he swung northward and hiked up near Jack Corbett's place, sank down on a shaded wall-bench and idly smoked.

Charley Barrett was across the road in front of *Turlock's Undertaking Parlour.* Charley, with his mild, sleepy look, was idling over there whittling with his Barlow knife. At the upper end of the roadway, where *Patterson's Apothecary Shop* cornered the square, Bert McKay was sitting in shade watching both sides of the southward roadway.

For a man, any man at all, involved or not involved, to pass unobserved the length of Plume's wide roadway, would have been impossible. For that reason when Terry Riley stepped out of his jailhouse, hitched at his shellbelt, looked north, looked south, then started walking toward Banning's place, four sets of alert eyes picked him up, caught the bright reflection of fading sunlight off his badge, and kept pace with his advance upon the saloon.

There were a few men in from the outlying ranches. It was too early, however, for the crowd of rangeriders to appear yet. At *Banning's Bar* men entered and left, mostly parched townsmen or travellers. There was a large freight train camped on the plain west of town; some of the flat-heeled, brawny men from that rough camp were also noticeable along the roadway. Some of them were in Banning's place too.

Afternoon steadily advanced towards evening. That promise of mid-summer sunblast which was beginning to manifest itself in the late spring days, gradually atrophied; there was a little rustling breeze, even, just before the shadows came, but it didn't last; it whimpered under overhang-eaves, scrabbled at loose windows, rattled a few tin roofs, then fled on southward out over the free-graze southward.

Gleeson killed his smoke, adjusted his belt, tipped back his hat and sat there looking. Watching and, he knew, being watched.

Terry Riley came back out of Banning's place, stood a little moment upon the opposite plankwalk, then stepped down and hiked over where Gleeson sat watching him approach.

"Understand you have a gun you're trying to make out belonged to Dean Furth," he said, confronting Gleeson. "Deputy; you're sure pushing for trouble, the way you've conducted yourself since you rode in here."

Gleeson moved only his eyes. "Tell me, Riley, who told you I had Furth's pistol?"

"You were at Maple Leaf today."

"I see. Well; one thing I'll say for Furth and Porter; they sure don't waste any time keeping their friends informed, do they?"

Riley rocked up onto his toes, rocked back down again. He considered Gleeson for a quiet moment from interested merry eyes. "You got no idea just how well informed their friends are, deputy," he said. "And you'd be surprised to know who their friends are."

This veiled alluding to the Morgans did not escape Gleeson at all, but he let Riley think it had. He said, "A bunch of pretty tough cowboys. I saw 'em out at Maple Leaf. I'll admit they stack up to pretty big odds for one man, Riley. The reason I said one man is because I'm pretty sure which side of the fence you'll be on."

"Then why don't you get smart, Gleeson. It's not too late to saddle up and head out."

"I thought I might do that—day before yesterday. Today—not a chance, Riley."

"You'd rather stay and be killed?"

Gleeson drew his legs up under him. He raised a knee, clasped both hands around it and said dryly, "I learned a long time ago Sheriff, this killin' business is a boot that fits both feet. Now you take the Maple Leaf rider who tried to draw on me—what was his name?"

"Andy Knight."

"Yeah. Now you take that Andy Knight—he hardly even saw it coming, and he thought he was a fair hand with a gun."

"That was just one man, Gleeson, remember that."

"Nope; there were four of 'em. They all could've drawn on me."

"This time there'll be five times that many, though. Gleeson; you're going to get it. You're too confident, too smart for your own good."

Gleeson put his head sceptically to one side. "You're threatenin' me," he softly said. "You're also saying there's going to be big trouble." He gently wagged his head at Sheriff Riley. "I haven't known many sell-out lawmen in my days, Riley, but of those I have known— you stand out as the one that makes me want to throw-up quickest. Walk along will you; go make your rounds, then take off your hat and bow low when Maple Leaf rides in, like a nice little traitor should do."

Riley's heavy shoulders dropped and his jaw locked hard. He was brick-red. Once more Gleeson had pushed him to the limit.

But this time Gleeson did not restrain himself as he'd done at the jailhouse when he'd wished to see Bannister. This time he unclasped his knee, gently lowered that leg and let his right hand lie easy on the bench within three inches of the saw-handle butt of his holstered sixgun. He was ready to kill.

Riley, despite his rage, recognized his peril. He had solid proof of how deadly that deputy U.S. marshal was with a gun, so he hung there fighting down his fury, turning it aside to feed upon something else, and he said, "I didn't threaten you, Gleeson, I promised you. You'll be dead before the sun sets this time tomorrow." He swung half around and went quickly away.

Gleeson watched Riley depart. He was bitterly smiling up around the eyes but his mouth remained firm and tough-set. He was aware of no one else within yards of him until Corbett's voice, speaking from the northward shadows of a recessed doorway, said, "Man; you almost went too far that time. You almost got yourself a gun-fight."

Gleeson turned, did not at once locate Corbett, and spoke while he was seeking him in the thickening evening. "Have you got that damned shotgun with you, Corbett?"

The barman stepped out. He had no visible gun at all. He moved closer to Gleeson's bench shaking his head. "Not armed," he said. "Just stepped out to have a breath of fresh air, saw you two and moved into a doorway just in case." Corbett halted, raised a foot and planted it upon the bench. He leaned there looking at Gleeson. "What're you waiting for?" he asked. Then said, "If I was in your boots I'm not sure I'd be sitting out here where everyone could see me, an' it getting dark."

Gleeson saw several men lope into Plume from the north. He did not reply to Corbett. Instead, he closely watched the oncoming riders. Corbett twisted his head, looked, and said, "Maple Leaf."

Gleeson recognized the men only when they swerved in at the rack in front of Banning's saloon. Neither Furth nor Dewey Porter were with them.

As though guessing Gleeson's thoughts, Corbett said, "Only three of 'em so far."

"So far?"

Corbett, still watching the rangeriders, shrugged. "The whole crew usually lopes in of an evening. That's only the tag end." Corbett returned his attention to Gleeson. "I've got a special customer in my backroom who'd like a few words with you," he said. "No hurry—this customer's real patient."

Gleeson shot the saloonman a look. Those yonder cowboys had trooped on into Banning's saloon; the roadway otherwise had reverted to its normal appearance. Barrett and McKay were still in sight. Bill Danvers was not, but Gleeson felt certain he'd be emerging from Banning's place any minute now. Things were gradually coming to a head.

"Can't see anyone right now," said Gleeson. "Maybe later. Who is it; what does he want?"

"It's a 'she', not a 'he', and she wants to talk to you."

"Mary? Mary Bonneville?"

Corbett's gaze was steady and grave. He nodded.

Gleeson pondered briefly. "Listen; go back in your place and keep out of the road. Make her do the same. Don't come out no matter what." At Corbett's widening look, his raised brows and his sudden abandoning of that relaxed, slouched-forward posture, Gleeson said, "I can't tell you any more than that, but do as I say."

There was a soft stillness, a gentle mantling of the yonder roadway, the roundabout buildings, with a pleasant pre-dawn murk. Lights were being lit here and there. Northward, over the spindle-doors at Corbett's saloon, an orange-yellow glow appeared.

"So it's here, finally," murmured Corbett, standing up straight. He sounded bitter. "All right, deputy. I wish you a lot of luck." He started to turn. "See you later." He strolled away, stopped near the entrance to his saloon and looked hard into the dusky north.

Gleeson was also peering that way. There was the muted, oncoming steady rumble of many riders passing southward into town. It was an ominous sound at any time, but tonight, to those knowing people who heard it, a chilling premonition seemed to precede it down Plume's roadway as far as *Banning's Bar.*

Gleeson watched that solid body of horsemen draw away from the darker night to become individual men on individual horses. He saw Dewey Porter first, big and bold and confident; he saw the mass of Maple Leaf riders swirl up around Porter and swing down. He was sure Dean Furth's father would be in that party but he never did make him out as those men tied up, came all together in a bunch upon the plankwalk, where they threw a careless look around, then swept

79

on into the saloon.

Now, at long last, strolling passersby began to sense something. Here and there people came briefly together to mutter, to pass on with quickened steps. It was almost as though an icy breeze had run the length of Plume's roadway.

A solitary girl walked north from the direction of the hotel. The little tap, tap, tap, of her shoes made an incongruous sound in this night where all other sounds were solid and menacing. Gleeson, shifting his attention after the men of the Maple Leaf were no longer in sight, caught that oncoming profile, the heavy upper thrust and the lower-down full-hipped sway. April Bannister. He ran his brows together, speculating. When she was close he said, "Have you been at the hotel?"

Until he spoke the girl, evidently deep in her own private thoughts, had not noticed him there in the dripping dark. He heard her breath catch, saw her start, and falter.

"It's Gleeson," he said. "The deputy U.S. marshal." Then repeated his question.

April took a wary step closer, looked at Gleeson's hat-brim-shaded face, and let her breath out. "No; I've been down to see Chet at the jailhouse."

"Was Sheriff Riley down there?"

April shook her head. "No, but the doors were unlocked. I just walked in."

Gleeson felt a coldness. "You mean the front door was open?"

"Yes; and that other door. The one leading into the cell-block, it was open too."

Gleeson faintly nodded over this. He thought it was

damned co-operative of Terry Riley to leave everything conveniently open like this. It made lynching a man so much neater if you didn't have to dynamite any doors. He said quietly, "How is your husband?"

April's heavy mouth drew down. "Like a caged animal, deputy. How would you be?"

"The same I reckon. Miss April; you're heading for Corbett's place aren't you?"

"Yes."

"All right, that's fine. You go along now, and you stay in there. I don't care what you hear—don't poke your head out again tonight."

April's mouth softened, her sultry gaze turned questioning and apprehensive. "What is it, deputy?" she murmured in a low, quick tone. "Is there going to be trouble tonight?"

Gleeson gently smiled. He also peremptorily jerked his head sideways. "Get inside, ma'm, and do like I told you—stay inside." He paused, then said, "Miss Bonneville's in there; you go keep her company. Go on!"

April, lashed by those last two words, swung and started off without another word. Gleeson watched her until there was nothing left to see.

Night time was fully down now, its velvet softness and its yielding fragrance enriching the world, making it deceptively mild and pleasant.

TEN

M EN CAME AND WENT, over at Banning's saloon. It didn't occur to Gleeson for some time after he'd observed this happening, that this was no chance event. Someone over there was sending men to recruit townsmen, cowboys from the other bars, and even those flat-heeled freighters from out at their westerly camp.

By the time Gleeson noticed that far more men were congregating at the saloon than were leaving it, this same occurrence had been noticed by others around town. Mostly, those who saw how this was going on, faded out of sight, going to their homes, there to be safely away from impending trouble.

Mary Bonneville left Corbett's place against the orders Gleeson had sent her, walked boldly south as far as Gleeson's vantage spot, halted and said softly to the deputy U.S. marshal, "Can't you see what they're doing over there? Can't you tell by the sounds someone is standing free drinks, stirring those men up?"

Gleeson looked into the cold, haughty face, drew his eyes into a slitted, reproving look, and jerked his head. "Get back to Corbett's and stay in there. I told him not to let you leave. What's the matter with you—don't you care whether or not you stop a slug? Lady; hell's going to bust loose here in this roadway any minute. Now you high-tail it back in there and don't let me catch you outside again."

"Deputy; we can organize the town's better element."

The beautiful, tall woman said rapidly, "Jack can leave through the rear—"

Gleeson abruptly stood up. His expression was cold and commanding. "I've never spanked anyone as big as you are but right now I'm damned close to tryin' it. Now you get under cover."

"You're alone, deputy; they'll kill you without—"

Gleeson reached out, grabbed Mary Bonneville's arm, swung her roughly and gave her a quick, strong push. "Get under cover."

Across the way a burly, large man had emerged from Banning's place. He walked to the very edge of the sidewalk and seemed to be idly smoking his cigar there. This faceless, hulking shadow had an ivory-butted sixgun that faintly shone in the night. Behind him, inside the saloon, was the steadily increasing tempo of loud, loose voices being profanely raised. The hitchracks around this big man were closely packed with saddled horses. Someone inside began to mutedly shout for silence.

Gleeson, his eyes never leaving that faceless square silhouette across the road, gave Mary Bonneville another rough shove. She swung back, her face white, her eyes enormous. "You fool!" she hissed at him, then went swiftly back the way she had come.

Gleeson moved away from his bench now; moved southward as far as the sunk-set door of a store, stepped into the total darkness of this little place and waited. Across the road that big man with the ivory-stocked gun flipped his cigar away, turned, and went casually strolling down toward the jailhouse.

Gleeson knew from this, that Danvers was satisfied the

time for the lynch-attempt was very near. He watched the U.S. Marshal go along to the jailhouse, push at the outer door, step inside and disappear from sight. Almost immediately after, the lamp Terry Riley had left burning, winked out, the jailhouse was plunged into full darkness, and Gleeson swung his gaze northward where Bert McKay and Charley Barrett had been. McKay was no longer up there by Patterson's shop. Barrett though, had not moved in the last hour. He was no longer whittling but he was over there with his shoulders upon the rough front wall of Turlock's undertaking establishment, and he was smoking. Gleeson saw the dull red tip of his cigarette occasionally glow and die down.

In Banning's place the noise became more raucous. Men were fiercely calling back and forth encouraging each other in this manner, but it was the solid undertone threaded through all the other noise which troubled Gleeson, for this was the sullen, angrily determined murmur of a mob.

Barrett tossed away his cigarette. It made an end-over-end, looping arc as it fell out into the roadway. Barrett straightened up off the wall, turned and started walking southward. Gleeson was the only one left now, Danvers, McKay, Charley Barrett would be preparing for war down at Terry Riley's building. He thought with uncharitable exultation of the surprise those men in Banning's saloon were going to get when they stormed that jailhouse.

Across the way several men pushed abruptly out onto the rough boardwalk. Gleeson felt the hair at the base of his skull stiffen at this sight. Those men were jumping the gun, but then, there always were those in every crowd who could not be restrained.

They stood over there glaring across towards Corbett's bar, but not quite at it, a little south of it toward that bench where Gleeson had been. He made a wry face about this; Terry Riley had sent those men out; he'd unquestionably sent them to find Gleeson.

The men proved at least the last part of this, when they stepped down into the dust and heavily started across, their course set for that empty bench, their swinging arms and rolling shoulders indicative of the kind of recklessness liquor inspires in men.

Gleeson shot a look southward and across to the jailhouse, then back again. He could not make it. He was well away from those walking men but the moment he stepped forth to walk away they'd see him. He dropped a hand, slightly raised his sixgun in its holster, dropped it back making sure it was riding loose, and waited. He was, for a short while at least, safe in his recessed doorway.

The trio of approaching men looked vaguely familiar, but until they broke up, separating a little as they came head-on toward the bench where Gleeson was supposed to be, he did not know them. Afterwards he did; it was those same three he'd fought once before very close to that same spot, only then there had been four of them.

Banning's saloon doors swung up, let two more men out along with a hot orange flash of inside light, then quivered closed again. But those two across the road did nothing; they sauntered to the plankwalk's edge and stood there, clearly with no intention of joining the three men whom they were watching.

"He ain't here," swore a lank cowboy with hair tumbling low across his forehead from under a pushed-back hat. "Terry was wrong."

Another cowboy looked around and back again. "He can't be far. He's got a room at the hotel, let's go look for him there."

The third rider seemed to Gleeson the least drunk of the three. He said scornfully, "Naw; what's the matter with you fellers anyway. He ain't goin' to get caught in a lousy hotel room with only one way out."

But the other two argued, saying that whether Gleeson was in his room or not they had to start their search somewhere, and the hotel being close, it was also the logical place to begin hunting.

The third man gave in sullenly, sourly saying, "All right, you damned idiots, but let's get this finished. I want to see the fun when they take Bannister out o' jail."

Gleeson had been hoping against hope those three would not start past for the hotel because they would go by within a foot or two of where he was flattened in the doorway. When those three men turned southward talking back and forth though, he knew a meeting was imminent. He shot a close look at those two across the way. Evidently, seeing the bench was empty and Maple Leaf's three riders were going to make a prolonged search, those two lost interest. They came together, spoke and softly laughed then returned to the saloon's interior. Gleeson breathed a sigh over this; he had thought, since neither of those men had appeared to have had anything to drink, they were two of the Morgan brothers.

The noise was no longer fierce-sounding over at Banning's, now it had sunk to that frightening rumble which preceded mob-action. Only one or two voices were raised; they cut sharply over that other sound giving orders and instructions and admonitions. Gleeson heard but scarcely heeded. He was listening to the on-coming long stride of those three Maple Leaf riders. His body turned cold, his brain became unusually receptive to every sound around him in the night, and his entire attention closed down upon those mingling bootsteps.

"Hey," a voice said just beyond Gleeson's doorway. "I need a drink. Let's go back and get us a bottle, then hunt up that lousy deputy marshal."

Someone just beyond Gleeson's doorway halted, cursed, and said, "That's the trouble with you, Sam; never finish nothing. Now go on. You want that bounty-money don't you? You heard Furth say he'd give a thousand for this Gleeson dead or alive, didn't you? Well then, dammit all, go on. You want some of them other fellers to get it?"

Sam muttered something but another of his companions joined in against him. This voice, Gleeson recognized, belonged to that stone-sober cowboy. "Oh shut up the both of you," he said disgustedly. "Now go on."

All three of them took several more onward steps, came out of the gloom parallel to Gleeson, and except for the sober man might have trudged right on past, but that one's eyes weren't fogged or glassy. He saw something man-shaped in doorway gloom, let a forced breath gush out and started to swing. Gleeson's gun flashed sideways raking this man brutally across the face from right to left. He cried out, put up both hands and staggered out into the roadway. His companions were dumbfounded. They didn't see Gleeson at once, they stared bewilderedly at the blinded man.

Gleeson caught the nearest one with an overhand swing crumpling him without a sound. The last man suddenly jumped clear. He did not understand what was happening, exactly, but he knew enough to try and get away from whatever it was. Gleeson went after him in a lunging rush.

The cowboy's right hand was clamped hard over his sixgun-butt when Gleeson struck him head-on with one shoulder battering the man off-balance, forcing him to fling out both arms for balance as he tripped over the plankwalk's edge and went sprawling into roadway dust.

But this man, although he'd dropped his gun, was sobered and frightened by Gleeson's attack; he rolled sideways, got both feet under him and sprang upright ducking under a sizzling right hand. He did not jump still farther away as Gleeson anticipated; he jumped in and caught Gleeson in the belly with a frantic blow. Gleeson grunted, halted and straightened up to suck air.

The cowboy rushed him flailing with both fists, hammered empty air and caught a savage strike in the left ribs that knocked him off course. He got his legs under him again, came around and stared, his breath coming on in broken gasps. He had never in his life been more sober than he was now. He measured Gleeson, pawed with a short jab, dropped his right shoulder behind a cocked fist and danced in, danced out, manœuvred around for a good position, and never got it.

Gleeson, made reckless by the imminence of having this fight discovered by someone coming out of Banning's saloon, rushed his opponent. But this cowboy was no ordinary barroom brawler, he was careful and he was experienced. Gleeson caught a bony fist in the left chest and another fist skidded along his cheekbone drawing blood. He had to jump away and begin circling. The Maple Leaf rider turned too, holding his ground, that cocked right fist ready, his white face tight from watchful concentration, his breathing audible.

They continued this circling until that blinded man, still clawing at his wrecked face where Gleeson's gunbarrel had savagely raked him, blundered too close, bumped the Maple Leaf man momentarily diverting him, then Gleeson dropped low, sunk his booted feet hard down into dust and catapulted forward throwing a powerful strike that went wrist-deep into the cowboy's middle forcing his breath out in a whistling rush.

The blinded man, knocked away by his friend's abrupt staggering, moaned and cursed. Gleeson passed him in a jump, caught the retching man over the bridge of the nose causing claret to spray, straightened him up enough to see how this man's eyes were aimlessly turning one way and another, and dropped him with a strike over the heart.

Of the original three Maple Leaf men only the one with both hands over his face was still upright, but that one was harmless to Gleeson. He nevertheless stripped all three of their guns, stepped back up onto the plankwalk, turned and was starting quickly away when across the road Banning's spindle-doors burst outward. Men spilled forth over there, some staggering, some only listing, and a few walking out stone sober.

It was one of the sober ones who saw Gleeson, saw that aimlessly staggering man and his two downed companions, and let off a high, sharp cry of rage and warning. At once someone fired from in front of Banning's place. Gleeson saw the crimson lash of that explosion and heard the slug strike six feet from him, tearing into wood siding. He turned and ran.

Men poured out into the roadway waving guns and shouting. Some ran on to that blinded cowboy, surrounded him yelling questions. Others knelt over the two unconscious men. For a space of several minutes these would-be assassins caused the mob to mill and aimlessly bump one another.

This was the time Gleeson needed. He got safely into the darkness opposite Riley's jailhouse, paused there to look back briefly, then he stepped clear and dashed across to the shielding gloom of the jailhouse overhang. He struck the door with a pistol barrel, barked his name, and when the door opened he burst inside.

ELEVEN

DECEPTIVELY SLEEPY-LOOKING Charley Barrett peered through jailhouse darkness at Gleeson and said, "Man; you got a knack for waitin' too long."

Gleeson called Barrett an uncomplimentary name, threw those three captured pistols upon Terry Riley's desk where Bill Danvers was sitting with a cup of coffee, and looked around.

McKay was standing to the right of the only window in the front wall. It had purposefully been made too small for a man's body to pass through it, then someone had protected the jailhouse against a break-out further, by having thick steel bars set into its mortar, up and down. All Gleeson could make out of McKay were his teeth. Bert was grinning over the little exchange between Gleeson and Barrett.

Danvers had his hat off. He waved casually towards a dark corner of Riley's office. "Get some coffee," he said to Gleeson. "There's a little stove over there. We made us a pot to keep from being bored to death."

"You won't be bored much longer," said Gleeson, for some reason he could not define, feeling irritated by the three indifferent men around him. "They're coming, Bill."

"Yeah, we know. Until you tried to whip 'em single-handed we were watching out the door. Go get yourself some coffee, Phil. This is likely to be one hell of a long night."

"Or an almighty short one," muttered Gleeson, feeling his way toward that stove Danvers had mentioned. "Looked like an awful lot of them to me."

"Phil, did you ever hear of a fight down in Texas called Adobe Walls?"

"Of course I've heard of it. But those aren't damned Indians out there either; they aren't goin' to be content to go ridin' around and around beatin' their chests and yelling."

Charley Barrett said, "Phil; your friend Riley is sure a helpful cuss. He left a rack of rifles an' shotguns an' six boxes of shells. 'You think they're goin' to walk through all that lead?"

Gleeson found the coffee pot, poured a tin cup full, tasted it, found the coffee bitter as lye, and felt his way back toward the others as he said, "Aw shuddup and keep watchin' out there." He halted near Danvers, sipped, made a face and put the cup aside. "You could float a horseshoe in that stuff."

Danvers lit a cigar and doused the light. He was thinking different thoughts. "I was telling Charley and Bert; just before I left Banning's place, Ralph Morgan came in out of the back alley."

"Did he know you?"

Danvers' teeth shone in the darkness. "I didn't wait to find out. That's when I eased through the crowd and walked out of there. You know, Phil, it made me feel good, seein' that weasel-faced, muddy-complexioned whelp here in Plume."

"I wonder if you'll be so happy about it a couple of hours from now, Bill."

Danvers' cigar gave off a grey puff. "I'll tell you something," he said quietly while the massive jailhouse walls smothered all that shouting and cursing northward up Plume's main roadway. "I never liked hunting; the kind where a feller locates a deer-run, finds himself a good position and sits down to wait until a buck comes slipping along on his way to water. Or antelope hunting either, where a feller hangs some white rags in the brush, then sits down and watches the curious little critters come up to sniff—then shoots them. That always turned my stomach, Phil. Now—if the deer and antelope were armed like I was—it might have appealed to me." Danvers slowly rose up from Riley's desk. "But this is different; *this* is my kind of hunting. Sure Phil; I'll be just as happy a couple of hours from now." He walked over where McKay was watching the roadway and peered out. His calm observation from over there drifted down to Gleeson.

"Looks like they're about ready to come pay us a visit boys. I'll tell you what we might do; we might help ourselves to Riley's shotguns and get a little ready."

The four of them crossed to a wall-rack, took down four sawed-off shotguns, silently loaded these murderous weapons, and afterwards spoke a little back and forth. Charley was disappointed the jailhouse only had one front window. Bert wondered about the mob breaking in through the cell-room. Phil Gleeson, who knew this could not be done, said so.

Danvers, still with that cigar between his teeth, looked over at Gleeson. "You better get that Bannister feller out of his cell all the same," he directed. "Someone could pot-shoot him in his cage through that high little barred window in the back-wall of his cell."

Gleeson, recalling that window, nodded and started for the steel-reinforced door separating Riley's office from the cell-block. Charley Barrett passed him Riley's ring of keys.

Bannister was hanging to the front bars of his cell when Gleeson came along to look in at him. The prisoner did not speak but his facial expression was full of mute pleading. Gleeson motioned him back, bent, unlocked the steel door and flung it back.

"Out," he commanded. "Walk ahead of me into the front office."

Bannister obeyed, all the youthful elasticity gone out of his limbs and his joints making him move jerkily. When Gleeson closed the steel-bound door, locked it and gestured ahead through the gloom, Bannister said, "They'll bust into this place like it was a rotten egg." Then he caught sight of three other men in the room watching him, and abruptly closed his mouth.

From over by the stove Charley Barrett said in a soft drawl, "Maybe. Maybe they'll do that, cowboy, but I'll promise you one thing—there'll be a pretty big pile of 'em that never quite make it." He held up a tin cup. "Care for some coffee?"

Bannister turned to put a perplexed look upon Gleeson. The deputy gestured for him to go after the coffee. He correctly interpreted Bannister's expression and said, "The U.S. Marshal and a couple more deputies. Now go get some coffee and keep out of the way."

Bannister went, his eyes already accustomed to the gloom, and mumbled politely when Barrett filled a cup and handed it to him. A little of the colour returned to Bannister's face but it was too dark to see this.

"Hey," Bert McKay softly called from over by the little window. "It looks like they're coming."

Barrett and Danvers stepped over for a long look. Danvers dropped his cigar, ground it out underfoot and hefted his shotgun. Gleeson, who did not go forward, saw Danvers do these things and knew from them that

McKay had been right.

Charley Barrett strolled over, had a look, strolled back by the stove, began to make a cigarette and said, "Must be fifty, seventy-five of 'em," finished the cigarette and lit it. "Good thing these are thick walls."

From a chair far back, unarmed Chet Bannister muttered: "I'd feel a sight better if there was a troop of horse-soldiers on the way."

No one paid Bannister any attention and he did not leave his corner.

Danvers cast an appraising look around. After so long a time in the dark it was possible to determine faces and expressions. He saw something arresting in the look of Gleeson and asked about it.

Phil went close, lowered his voice and said, "We made a blunder, Bill. A bad one, I think."

Danvers, after ten years, knew Gleeson never dramatized. He said quickly, "What; out with it man!"

"Bannister's wife, Bill. She and a saloonman who's been helpful, and the woman who gave me Furth's pistol—the lot of them are up at Corbett's saloon. It won't take very long after the Morgans, Furth and Porter discover they aren't just going to walk in here after Bannister, for one of them to figure how to get him out without a fight."

"Yeah? How they goin' to bring that off, I'd like to know. If they think we'll trade Bannister for his wife they're backin' the wrong horse."

"Bill; they'll kill her."

Danvers scoffed at this, but after a little time had passed and Gleeson's expression did not soften, Danvers said, "They wouldn't. Listen; drunk or not, there are a lot of plain rangemen out there. They'd never hold still for a woman bein' shot down."

"That," contradicted Gleeson, "is exactly how they could do it. When the firin' starts and everything is confused and shadowy—she'd stop a stray one—and they'd use it against us, Phil. Furth or his rangeboss would swear up and down it was our bullet."

Danvers was briefly silent again while more of his stubbornness crumpled. "But maybe that saloonman's smart enough to figure all this out. Maybe he's already got himself and those two women hidden."

"Where?"

"How the hell would I know where?" exploded Danvers, as he twisted to cock an ear at the nearing clamouring of what was clearly audible now, thick walls or no thick walls; the curses and roarings of that drunken lynch-mob. "Anyway, it's too late to do anything about, Phil. Get over to the window with Bert."

Gleeson teetered there undecided on what course to pursue even after Danvers crossed to the front door with his shotgun. Someone outside made up Gleeson's mind for him, they threw a stone through the little barred window showering Bert McKay with glass. Bert swore with feeling, stepped back to shake splinters off, and Gleeson went forward, poked his shotgun between the bars, cocked one barrel and fired it high.

That throaty roar had its instantaneous effect. Shouting, gesticulating men out in the exposed roadway keened in sudden fear, beat against each other and broke fleeing for cover.

A tall, slatternly-looking man with two pistols, one in each hand, stood wide-legged cursing the mob. Bert McKay stepped up close at the sound of that man's voice, peered out, said, "Cal Morgan," and jerked his shotgun up.

But Morgan passed over into a crowd of milling, armed men and was at once lost to sight. McKay twisted to tell Danvers whom he had seen. From his position half way along the northward wall Danvers barked an order at Barrett: "Charley; come over here and ease this damned door open a fraction while I lie down and peek out. If the Morgans are out there—remember what I said—we want them first."

Gleeson looked down where big Bill Danvers was letting himself down. Charley Barrett came up and Gleeson said, "Don't you open that door, Charley."

Both Barrett and Danvers swung. Barrett seemed tractable but Danvers' eyes flashed. "I give the orders in here," he snarled. "You just mind your damned window."

Gleeson said once more: "Charley, don't you open that damned door!"

A hail of lead struck the jailhouse front. A goodly proportion of those slugs quivered into the door making it buck and shake upon its hangers. Bert McKay looked harassedly around. "You heard him," he said to Charley. "Get away from the door, they're concentrating on it."

This was true. Lead flattened against steel strap-hinges as though by design someone out there was directing gunfire in such a way as to tear the door loose. All the defenders inside understood the thinking here; if that door could be tumbled out into the roadway, systematic ground-sluicing by half a hundred guns would inevitably kill every man inside. It was not a new tactic at all, but it had proven itself a very effective one in a hundred similar battles the width and length of the gunfighting West.

Even Bill Danvers had to get away when bullets began coming through shredded wood. He was fighting mad now too.

Gleeson rubbed shoulders with Bert. When it was possible to do so, these two took quick looks outward. Generally though, nearly as much gunfire was being concentrated against the little window as was being poured into the solid oaken door.

Charley Barrett ambled over, stood back to one side and waited for a lull to say, "Never mind aimin'. Just poke your barrels out and fire into 'em."

McKay, sweating and bleeding from several minor glass scratches, ducked down, shot Charley a look, and said, "Somewhere I've heard about their always bein' a hell of a lot of generals and never too many soldiers in situations like this. Why don't you go take a flyin' leap at a ghost and leave the fightin' to them as knows how."

Charley grinned, eased over to shoulder Bert away, poke his shotgun fully out and yank off both barrels. The recoil almost knocked him flat. It almost deafened Gleeson who turned and heartily cursed Barrett.

McKay resumed his former place and Charley, content that he'd demonstrated his tactic, re-loaded shotguns and passed them to the two men manning the window.

For a long time this blind-firing continued. Because they were fully occupied Gleeson nor Barrett nor

McKay paid any attention to Bill Danvers. Not until a shuddering shotgun blast erupted northward along the front wall did they look in that direction.

Danvers had enlarged a shredded place in the door, had pushed his shotgun through and was firing blindly. Whether it was this devastating gunfire from the defenders, or the more probable dawning suspicion of the attackers out in the dark roadway that one deputy U.S. marshal could not possibly be doing all the firing, no one ever knew for certain, but regardless, that roadway gunfire began to dwindle as attackers backed off to regroup and talk.

TWELVE

F IRST BLOOD," muttered Gleeson, stepping back from the wrecked window, going over to pocket more shotgun shells. Across the table where he was also getting shells, Bill Danvers looked at Gleeson from under lowered brows. But Bill said nothing; Gleeson had been right about not opening that door. They all knew this now.

" 'Saw Cal Morgan too," stated Bert McKay, sauntering up for more shells. "Cal and Ralph. That means sly Moe is somewhere close by." McKay peered over at Bannister in his corner. "Four cups of coffee," he ordered. "An' make it snappy, boy."

Bannister got up. He went to the stove, stood looking downward without raising a hand, and said, "The damned pot's got a hole near the bottom. All the java's run out." He swung toward Bill Danvers. "Let me get into this too, Marshal. I can handle a gun."

Gleeson said dryly, "Yeah; that's why the lot of us are bottled up in here—because you can handle a gun. Go on back and sit down and keep out of the way."

Danvers nodded agreement without even looking around. Bannister turned and sullenly returned to his chair.

For a little while those men outside did not fire a single shot and this increasingly worried the defenders although none of them mentioned it until Charley Barrett said, "You suppose they're makin' a batterin' ram?"

Danvers grunted dissent but otherwise said nothing. Gleeson returned to the window, peeked out and drew away seconds ahead of a sniper's shot. He said casually, as though that bullet had not come within a breath of puncturing his skull, "Getting smart now, those stupid cowboys. They're atop the buildings across the way. You can't see a one of them."

The silence ran on, much more perilous in its implications than the earlier gunfire had been. Clearly, someone out there was up to something. Then it came, the unmistakable reedy voice of Sheriff Terry Riley.

"Gleeson—an' whoever else is in there with you—come out. Come out or get blown out!"

Gleeson and Danvers had the same thought. Both jumped toward the cell-block door. McKay and Barrett, not yet comprehending, stood and watched. Danvers got the lock opened and was straightening up to yank the door back, when a tremendous explosion rocked the jailhouse, upended furniture, knocked racked guns to the floor and tumbled the riddled and useless coffee pot to the floor.

That cell-block door, already released from its latch, swung with terrific force against Marshal Danvers, who had just stepped back two long steps to swing it back. He did not get the full violent impact, but he got enough of a blow to knock him backwards over a little table, breaking this piece of furniture and dumping the marshal in a limp heap better than half way across the room.

Outside, before the clouds of dust even began settling back, before the stunning detonation was cleared from five totally unexpecting minds, the gunfire started up again.

McKay and Barrett sprang to the window but Phil Gleeson ignored that shooting to bend down, catch hold of Bill Danvers and drag him into a safe, dark corner. He spent only a moment with Danvers; just long enough to ascertain that there was no bleeding from the nose or ears, then crossed swiftly to the cell-block door, poked his head around it, and erupted into a wild fit of coughing from cordite fumes.

The cells were twisted and broken almost beyond recognition. Whatever had caused that fierce explosion, except for some inordinately thick partitioning walls, would most assuredly have collapsed the jailhouse around and over its defenders.

Gleeson could see little other than the ruin because of mingling smoke and ancient dust. He slammed the door, locked it, and leaned against it choking back more fits of coughing.

Bannister called from his corner: "Deputy; what was it?"

McKay and Barrett also looked toward Gleeson, this identical question plain on their sweat-shiny, strained faces.

"Damned if I know," replied Gleeson, rubbing his profusely watering eyes. "Dynamite maybe, but it sure wrecked things in there."

Bannister sprang up, his mouth twisting in an ugly look. "They got 'em," he cried out. "I heard Riley tellin' someone last week right after he locked me up, that they got some howitzer shells left over from when the last army column was here."

Gleeson squinted his burning eyes. It was on the tip of his tongue to make Bannister repeat that but he never got the chance. Several riflemen opened up from somewhere across the road, overhead. Their slanting gunfire at once drove McKay and Barrett to their knees as bullets sang downward into the office.

"Hey deputy," a reedy voice yelled out. "Hey you fellers in the jailhouse—how did you like that little surprise? Listen; we got seven more o' them shells. You come out with Bannister or you get every one of 'em."

Gleeson heard Danvers moan and felt his way around the little broken table to his side. Danvers was coming out of it; he was throwing his arms around as though groping for something to support his considerable weight with. Gleeson caught one hand and held it. Danvers came up into a sitting position but it was a little while before his drifting eyes settled into a focusing pattern. Then Gleeson told him what had happened and Danvers nodded.

"Through that little high window in the cell where

Bannister was," he mumbled thickly. "Sure as hell. We should have anticipated that. Help me up, Phil."

Gleeson did; he eased Danvers down upon a bench and retrieved the marshal's guns, put them upon the bench at his side and listened as another attacker shouted curses at the lawmen inside Terry Riley's jailhouse.

McKay raised up suddenly at the window, shoved out his shotgun and let off both barrels. As had previously happened with Barrett, the recoil nearly knocked Bert flat. He shook himself, bent to reload as sniper-bullets struck in through the same window, buried themselves in the yonder wall with a ripping sound, and said, "Charley, did you ever consider givin' up your evil ways an' settlin' down on a nice farm somewhere?"

Barrett made a ragged smile, said, "Right now I'm thinkin' o' that mighty serious, Bert," and drew in closer to the front wall so none of those stray shots could reach him.

Gleeson got a dipper full of water for Danvers from a wooden bucket over by Bannister. As he did this the younger man spoke in anguish to him.

"It's not worth gettin' four men killed over, deputy. I'll walk out there."

"The hell you will," growled Gleeson. "I might have favoured that an hour back, but now this is a sort of personal thing. Like I told you, Bannister; you sit there and keep quiet."

Danvers drank, coughed, spat and gently shook his head. "What the hell hit me?" he asked.

"That steel-bound door."

Danvers looked over, swiped at his eyes to clear away

the fogginess, and felt around for his guns. "Thought I'd been stomped by an elephant," he muttered, and shakily stood up. "Phil; did I hear you right a minute ago—did you say they had some more of those howitzer shells?"

"Yeah you heard right, Bill. Seven more."

Danvers drained the last of the water from the dipper, spat again and after that seemed to recover rapidly. "We got to watch the back then," he said. "We got to watch close too. It won't take seven more to bring this cussed building down around our ears."

Gleeson nodded, took up his shotgun and started away. At the cell-block door he twisted to look back. Bert and Charley were watching him. He tossed them a little salute and they both grinned back at him.

Inside the cell-block breathing was both painful and difficult. Additionally, there was a hole where that little window had been large enough for two men to climb through abreast. In front of it was the tangled wreckage of Bannister's former cell.

Gleeson made his way carefully through the debris, tugged free what remained of Bannister's bunk, propped this against the wall and gingerly climbed up until he could see out.

The night was faintly lighted now by a belated, sickle moon. Out in the empty alleyway lingering clouds of dust and smoke hung in the still atmosphere. It was difficult around here to make out more than the louder, erupting guns around in the main roadway. Light weapons sounded like distant hand-claps.

The tickling sensation cordite causes bothered Gleeson. He had no doubt that somewhere back here, were armed men. If he coughed it could cause an eruption of shots. He particularly wished for whoever was out there to believe all the jailhouse-defenders were still in Riley's front office.

Some ten minutes after he'd improvised his firing platform from Bannister's wrecked wall-bunk, his surmise about attackers being in the alleyway was confirmed. He saw a small man dart between two onward buildings. A moment later another man also ran across this same opening. When a third man made this identical crossing carrying something which seemed to weight him forward, Gleeson reached down for his holstered sixgun and put the shotgun carefully, noiselessly aside.

He had no doubts about what that third man was carrying; it made his blood turn cold at the thought of being in the obvious and only opening into the jailhouse where those attackers would try to throw that second howitzer shell.

For a while only the popping of guns around front broke the stillness of this threatening night. Gleeson strained to pick up movement in his area. When there was nothing to see he worried. Clearly those three men and their highly explosive, short-fused shell, were also rummaging the gloom for movement, for any suspicious sight or sound, before they made their run on the jailhouse.

He drew faint comfort from the obvious fact that in order to get close enough to heave the shell inside, those three attackers would have to race across the alley's unobstructed width. At least one of them would, and as heavy as that shell was, he thought this would be the largest of those three men, which was, in Gleeson's view, a fortunate thing. The larger the man the easier he'd be to hit in the dark.

But no large man came charging forth. Not even a small man. There was just the emptiness, the stillness, and the popping of guns around front.

Something blurred where an old shed stood gently decaying, slightly apart from a large horsebarn and a log granary. Gleeson blinked, held his straining eyes upon that spot, held his breath and waited. Perseverance proved its own reward; he saw two shapes drift together in a black curving of a warped old wall. Shortly after, a third shape glided in, this one larger, more bent than the other shapes.

Gleeson cocked his handgun, carefully rested it upon a jagged piece of blasted jailhouse wall, tracked those blurs and held steady upon them. But for another draggingly long period of time there was no movement. He was beginning to worry that, some way, those three men had crept away, had eluded him completely, when wet moonlight eerily shone in a dull way off a gun barrel. That was all Gleeson could make out of those three men, so well had they chosen their place of concealment, but it was enough to reassure him. He let his breath out, steadied his gun-hand, and waited.

Sweat ran under his shirt. It trickled down from his forehead. But when one of those men raised up, spread his legs and took a solid stance while another man bent across something that taller man was holding, Gleeson forgot his dread and his discomfort. He did not understand exactly what the shorter man was doing, but he completely understood *why* he was doing it. Somehow, the shorter man was activating the fuse of a howitzer shell!

Suddenly the shorter man wheeled away. The tall man lunged forward towards the alley in a clumsy but determined, almost desperate run, and his companions back in darkness both began abruptly to fire toward the ruptured wall where Gleeson stood.

It almost worked. Two bullets struck stunningly below Gleeson showering him with stinging pieces of dirt and mushrooming little clouds of dust. Gleeson flinched, blinked and forced himself to desperately seek out the running man. He laid a shot forward, missed narrowly and when the running man faltered, evidently surprised at that onward muzzleblast, Gleeson shot again. This bullet struck its target. The big man stumbled, caught his balance, teetered out there for a second or two, then, probably no longer mindful of the lethal load in his arms, swung heavily around and went unsteadily back the way he had come.

Gleeson did not fire again. He stared, fascinated, completely forgetful of his dangerously exposed position as that panting and wounded attacker stumbled back towards his companions. They cried out when it dawned upon them that the short-fused shell was bearing down upon them. They broke and ran. Gleeson tracked one, fired, missed, then stood open-mouthed as that man swung around, dropped to one knee and deliberately put three successive shots into his cohort, the man with the howitzer shell.

But it was too late, this belated action. As the big man

fell, the howitzer shell exploded. Gleeson, anticipating this a moment before the big man went down drunkenly, lurching along, stumbling lower and lower, shot fatally but unwilling to surrender his life this easily, crouched close to what remained of the rear jailhouse wall.

He had his eyes closed but the brightness got under the lids. It burnt a searing shade of yellow-orange across his brain. The detonation seemed to suck away all air. Gleeson gasped and choked. Sound waves broke against his protecting wall, pushed through and over, where the jagged hole was over Gleeson's head, and filled the world with their ear-splitting crash.

Steel fragments too whistled in the night, and somewhere beyond Gleeson's crouched position, a building creaked and groaned and collapsed with a terrific sound of splintering timber, tinkling glass and whiplashing boards.

Even the echoes were deafening as they ran on endlessly through the northward night. But normalcy eventually returned, and with it came the incongruous yapping of a little dog inside a house not too far distant.

When he dared, Gleeson rose up and peeked out. There was nothing left to be seen of those three men, but what shocked him most was that, although that massively sturdy log granary was demolished, the listing, decaying old shed seemed not to have been disturbed at all.

THIRTEEN

B ILL DANVERS RAN into the cell-block looking
frantically for Gleeson. When he found him,
beginning to rise up out of his protective crouch,
Danvers was relieved.

Gleeson explained what had happened. Danvers
looked out, stepped back and shook his head. He seemed
about to say something but he didn't, he beckoned to
Gleeson then moved back toward the front office with
Gleeson following him.

McKay and Barrett were still manning their bullet-
scored little window. Danvers went over where they
were, got down on one knee and jerked his head at
Gleeson, in this way telling Gleeson to join the others.
When the four of them were together against the front
wall Danvers raised his voice above that outside gunfire
and said, "Boys, we've got to get out of here. They failed
at tossing the second shell in, but they still have six more
of those infernal things, and look around you—this
building can't take another inside blast without coming
down."

McKay and Barrett had, up until now, occasionally
joked back and forth, confident of their safety inside
Riley's jailhouse. Now though, neither of them had a
word to say.

Danvers looked at his deputies, read their faces correctly and nodded in agreement with what he saw. "Not
much of a chance for us out there. But if we stay in here
there's no chance at all, an' for myself I'd rather go down

shootin' than be trapped like a rat under tons of wood and adobe."

He looked at Gleeson. "You know this town the best— what's our best bet once we're clear of the jailhouse?"

Gleeson considered this carefully, then said, "Jack Corbett's saloon, I reckon. At least it'll do until they decide to fling one of those shells in there too." He paused to consider each attentive face. "The trouble will be gettin' up there. It's at the other end of town."

"Phil," spoke up Charley Barrett. "They're out in the back alley too, aren't they?"

Gleeson nodded. "They were, and I expect they still will be. When we leave we'll have to stay close together. If they can separate us we won't stand a chance."

Danvers looked from one to the other of them. "We'll do as Phil says, we'll stay close and we'll try and make it up to Corbett's place. Phil, you'll lead out."

The four of them exchanged a solemn look, then that roadway gunfire attracted their attention with its increasing ferocity again and Barrett gingerly rose up, awaited a slight lull and peered out. He did not pull back as swiftly as he had other times. McKay growled at him to get his head down. Barrett obeyed but not right away, and he said, as he did obey, "There's something going on over across the road. I couldn't see 'em very well, but it looked like six or seven fellers comin' together over there. We better not try leavin' until we're plumb sure they aren't figurin' some kind of a trap."

The others agreed with this and moved away to resume their defence of the front wall. Gleeson and Danvers got to the riddled front door, were readying their weapons there when Bert McKay called electrically from over by the little window.

"Hey; look atop that building across the road. They've went and made a sort of catapult out of a springy pine board. They got one of those damned howitzer shells lashed back on the board."

Gleeson dropped down, set one eye to a jagged hole in the door and strained to see. Fortunately those men atop the onward building were easily sky-lined. What he saw made his blood chill. Exactly as McKay had described it, the attackers had improvised a means for lobbing another of those shells against the jailhouse.

"Rifles," cried Gleeson, springing up and springing across towards the gun-rack. "Sixguns won't do it and neither will shotguns. Use rifles."

All of them hurriedly armed themselves with carbines from Riley's wall-rack. Danvers got back to the door when Gleeson already had his gunbarrel poked through to sight along it. In fact Danvers was the last one to open up. Gleeson fired first, then McKay and Barrett fired, and last, Bill Danvers got off his opening round.

At once a furious return-fire came back. The fight steadily increased in ferocity. Men were shouting beyond the jailhouse. The defenders ignored everything but those suddenly agitated figures overhead, working with their improvised catapult. Two men up there on the roof went down; one of them bounded to the roof's edge, flopped momentarily there, plunged over and fell heavily into the roadway.

Gleeson and his companions were excellent gunshots. Within moments that catapult was completely abandoned. The pine board stood incongruously upright with a howitzer shell lashed to it, but with no one anywhere around to activate the shell or bend back the board.

Danvers withdrew his carbine, levered it open, peered into the empty chamber and started after shells. Gleeson still had two rounds left. He called for Bill to fetch him back a handful of cartridges and did not relinquish his vigil.

A number of men came racing down out of the building across the road and one of them recklessly burst out onto the plankwalk. Gleeson caught this man over his sights and fired. The man, scarcely more than a pitch black shape against the only slighter building front, jerked, flung out his arms, dropped a pistol and let out a shrill cry. From over at their window Barrett and McKay also fired at this man. He went down, rolled off the plankwalk and flattened where soft moonlight shone upon his upturned face.

"Riley," said Gleeson, surprised into speaking aloud. "That was Sheriff Riley. See that reflection off his chest; that's his badge."

"He did it no honour," barked Bert McKay, then gasped as another man tried sprinting away from the same doorway Riley had used.

Danvers fired at this man, missed and fired again. But the fleeing man jumped into a narrow passageway between two buildings and was lost to sight.

McKay said bitterly, "Ralph Morgan, dammit. You shot too fast, Bill."

Danvers did not comment.

Red flashes of light began erupting from dozens of different places again as the roadway attackers, aware that the catapult scheme had been defeated, angrily resumed their direct, frontal firing.

Gleeson systematically aimed at eliminating their enemies by simply holding his fire until the second after one of them fired, then throwing lead slightly below the muzzleblast. Once at least a man tumbled through a store window across the way and flopped face down across the boardwalk as a result of this kind of firing.

But again someone was directing a steady fire against the jailhouse door, driving both Gleeson and Danvers away. Lead began to rip downward again too, from across the way where prone riflemen were firing in through the little window.

McKay and Charley Barrett, once again compelled to crouch against the wall below their vantage point, reloaded and patiently waited out the worst of this lead storm. Over in his corner Chet Bannister, the safest of them all, was beside himself with agitation. He called upon Danvers and Gleeson both for permission to join the fighting. Neither of them answered him.

"She's gettin' hot," Danvers shouted at Gleeson, forced to raise his voice to be heard at all. He had his mouth open to say more when out of nowhere a bullet came blindly seeking and ripped a four inch gash along the Marshal's ribs. He winced, spun unsteadily from impact and dropped his carbine.

Gleeson saw the blood gush and jumped over bearing Danvers away from there over toward the comparative safety of the north wall. There, he bent to examine the wound. He straightened up with relief and said, "You'll make it. No busted ribs, just a bad cut."

Danvers peered downward, swore and tore the lower half of his shirt, handed this to Gleeson to make a bandage of, and dourly said, "We've got to clear out of here, Phil. This place is getting like a steel ball; a man shoots into it and the bullet goes bouncing around until it hits something."

Gleeson worked swiftly, fashioning an adequate bandage and saying nothing until he had finished. Danvers' wound was not serious although it had profusely bled, but what Danvers had said was very true and Gleeson knew it. Bullets now came through that dangerously weakened front door without encountering any serious opposition. And if this wasn't bad enough, there was the very strong possibility that their enemies might decide to try lobbing another of their howitzer shells in through the shattered cell-block wall. If they managed to succeed at this, as Danvers had observed earlier, the weakened building would very likely collapse, burying them all.

He nodded at the U.S. Marshal. "We'll give 'em a volley then head out the back way, Bill."

Before Danvers could agree Bert McKay's abrupt profanity rang out and Gleeson, thinking McKay had been hit, spun around. But McKay and Barrett both were staring out their window. Beyond in the roadway, several men yelled in what sounded to Gleeson like genuine alarm.

"What is it?" Danvers loudly asked. "Bert; Charley; get away from that damned window. What is it?"

Barrett stepped back first, then McKay. Barrett said in an astonished tone of voice: "I had Cal Morgan in my sights. I pulled the trigger—and the blasted carbine was empty. But hell—Cal went down anyway. Went down over there behind an overhang post and you can see him lyin' out there in the gutter."

For a moment no one said anything. McKay solemnly nodded confirmation of Barrett's words. "I saw it. I heard Charley's gun click empty." Those two looked dumbfounded.

Danvers growled at them, "We got no ghost riders helpin' us, you pair of idiots. Someone—"

"Corbett," barked Gleeson. "Corbett's over there behind 'em somewhere. It had to be someone behind Morgan and the others."

Out in the roadway men began shouting back and forth. Gleeson was apparently not the only one who suddenly realized there was an enemy lurking among the attackers, somewhere in the shadowy night, and this worked its understandable demoralising magic upon the sobering rangemen. Their gunfire began to diminish while their shouts increased.

Gleeson risked going over to the riddled door for a look outward. He saw indistinct man-shapes whipping backwards from exposed positions. He also saw a long-legged individual make a rush for the sprawled body of Cal Morgan in the roadway. Working fast, too fast, Gleeson ran his gun out and fired at that man, believing him to be one of the other Morgans. The slug struck two feet short, peppered the running man with dirt and forced him to swing back and go racing back to cover.

Several return-shots drove Gleeson away from the door again. Danvers came up to him saying, "If that was your friend the saloonman, he's taking a bad chance. They'll hunt him down."

Gleeson ignored Danvers to gesture for Bannister, McKay and Barrett to come back where he and Danvers stood. In explanation of this he said to Danvers, "I think I know why Corbett did that—to divert them out there long enough for us to get out of here. At least we're going to figure it that way." He turned, striking out for the cell-block door. Bannister ran up to him with a Winchester carbine in his fist and a sixgun in his heretofore empty holster. Bannister reached for the door first. Gleeson, seeing Bannister's armament, hung fire a second, then shrugged and nodded for the younger man to swing the door back.

From here on this was to be as much Bannister's fight as anyone else's; let him have the guns. With Bannister's back to him Gleeson turned, saw McKay and Barrett exchanging a look with Bill Danvers, and said, "He's got a right to defend himself, hasn't he?"

The other three solemnly nodded, ended this phase of their fight for survival without a word, and pushed on into the devastated cell-block behind Gleeson.

FOURTEEN

GETTING OUT of the wrecked jailhouse was surprisingly easy. Gleeson thought it was entirely too easy; he did not believe, even after all five of them were safely across the alley and into the protective dark shadow of that sagging, decaying old building over there, that this could have been accomplished without discovery.

"It's got to be that they're all fearful over having an assassin among them," Gleeson said to Danvers.

Danvers, unconcerned about the reason for their easy escape from the jailhouse, said only, "Lead out away from here, Phil, and make it fast."

They glided off westerly, away from the alleyway but parallel to it. They crossed darkened rear-yards, halted in the shadow of sheds, barns, even an open-sided hen-roost once, on their northward way. Gleeson led them back toward the alley when they encountered an impossibly tall, solid wooden fence. Here, they could look the full distance of the liverybarn from back to front. Gleeson considered crossing through that wide runway. It would put them upon the west side of the central thoroughfare and only a little south of Corbett's place, which was not only on across the roadway but was also several doors northward.

Danvers, uneasy and restless, said, "Go on, Phil; so far so good."

Gleeson looked around, counted the shadows around him, stepped out and darted ahead. Behind him the others fled swiftly the alleyway's dark width and faded out inside the barn too, fanning out, flattening in total darkness scarcely breathing.

The gunfire southward along the road was increasing again, as though the jailhouse-attackers were making a particularly aggressive assault.

"They probably think we've been whittled down," opined Charley Barrett to Bert McKay at his side in the barn. Gleeson, ten feet away, heard this and privately agreed with it.

Danvers scouted the barn as far as the harness-room, returned and hissed for the others to come along. Bannister was the last man to move out; he seemed worried over that empty alleyway out back and the doorless wide opening leading inside from it. As Bannister slipped along he kept peering over his shoulder apprehensively.

But nothing interrupted the progress of those five men until, just beyond the harness-room, Danvers raised his carbine signalling for the others to remain where they were while he scouted forward again. Everyone but Gleeson obeyed; Gleeson went ahead with Danvers, dropped to one knee at the front opening, poked his head out and around and remained that way for a long time.

It was possible to see men southward, flattened against building fronts where they could not be seen from within Riley's office. Most of these men had smoking sixguns in hand.

Across the road, also out of sight of anyone inside Riley's jailhouse, stood a dozen or so men. Gleeson watched that band wondering about them; they seemed to have lost their taste for the hard fighting. Every one of them was armed yet none of them made any attempt to join the furious onslaught which was nearing some kind of a wild crescendo, southward.

Danvers edged over beside Gleeson. He bobbed his head northward where darkness lay heavy. "Is that Corbett's place?" he asked. Gleeson nodded, still watching that clutch of spectators across the way.

"We can't risk runnin' for it though as long as those fellers are standin' over there, Bill."

118

Danvers' attention swung. He considered the dozen non-combatants a moment, twisted half around and flagged for the others to hasten up. "You and I," he said to Gleeson, "will take care of that." When Barrett, Bannister and McKay dropped down close by Danvers turned to them. "You boys give us cover-fire if it turns out we need it. Phil and I're goin' to walk out of here bold as brass, hike across where those men are standing, and either bag us a big catch or wind up in one hell of a fight."

Gleeson, listening to Danvers, thought it just might work. The roadway was full of confusion, the night was dark enough to make identifying others uncertain, and most of the attention was rivetted on the battered jailhouse where gunfire cut away wood, pocked the front wall, and made it unlikely, had anyone been in the building, that they would have dared raise up to return that savage fire.

Danvers tapped Gleeson's shoulder. The pair of them rose up, stepped forth and started walking ahead side by side. Once away from the barn Gleeson resisted a powerful impulse to look southward and see what the jailhouse looked like to its attackers. Danvers looked but Gleeson never did; he kept his whole attention upon that silent, shadowy group of men they were approaching.

When they were twenty feet off several of those men turned indistinct, white faces to gaze upon Gleeson and Danvers. When they halted ten feet off several more men looked around. When Gleeson spoke every one of those men jerked around, and it was possible then to see how their eyes popped wide and their jaws sagged.

"Drop those guns!"

Danvers backed up Gleeson's command by cocking his low-held Winchester and swinging it a little, back and forth.

"Drop 'em!"

Guns fell. The men upon the plankwalk were speechless. They were paralysed at this wholly unexpected appearance of the man whom they recognized as Gleeson, and whom they had up until this moment believed must certainly be either dying in the jailhouse or so pinned down by gunfire he could not even fire back.

Danvers stepped up close and let overhang gloom engulf him. Gleeson gestured with his gun. "Walk," he said. "Head for Corbett's place. Make one wrong move and you'll never make another. *Walk!*"

Danvers hung back, let Gleeson herd their captives onward a short distance, then stepped out, flagged across the road, stepped back and went along in Gleeson's wake.

Bannister, McKay and Barrett darted across the road. Southward other men were beginning to boldly rise up, to boldly expose themselves as they steadily advanced upon the jailhouse keeping up that devastating gunfire. The attention of all those attackers was fixed ahead on Terry Riley's battered jailhouse; they scented victory and were hastening to implement it. If any of them looked northward and made out that dark body of walking men, they did not see anything particularly wrong for there were no calls, no shots.

Gleeson drove the captives into Corbett's bar, stepped around them, wig-wagged for them to line up along the wall, and called for Barrett and McKay to complete the disarming process. Up until now not a one of those men had spoken. Now one did. He was a cowboy, by the looks of him, and he was stone-sober.

"Listen, deputy; we had no big part in it. We come into town a little while back when the fightin' was hot, an' sort of drifted down there to watch."

Charley Barrett stepped back with several pistols. He opened the gate of one of these guns, spun the cylinder, closed the gate and tossed the gun backwards. He was cynically smiling at the spokesman for those riders.

"Four shot-out chambers in that gun," he announced. "Naw; you fellers had no big part in it." Charley called the rangeriders a bad name. "Turn around," he snarled. "Step back from that wall, put your hands over your damned heads and lean forward." When this order had been obeyed Charley looked around at Danvers and Gleeson. "Crack 'em over the head or tie 'em up?" he asked.

Gleeson spoke ahead of Danvers. "Neither, Charley; let Bannister have 'em. They wanted to hang him, so let him guard 'em." Gleeson looked around at Bannister. "Do what you want," he said, "so long as you don't kill 'em in cold-blood."

Bannister brusquely nodded, stepped forward and prodded his prisoners with a carbine barrel. "Stand steady," he barked. "And when it gets to hurtin', leanin' like that, just keep right on leaning because the first man who moves will be tryin' to escape, in my view."

Danvers, watching those twelve captives, frowned in concentration. "Phil," he said to Gleeson. "We could get some more like that. In all this excitement no one knows who is who out there. What do you think?"

Whatever Gleeson had to say to this proposition was postponed; a blast exploded out in the southward roadway that made every window in Corbett's saloon quiver in its casement. The walls shook and the overhead unlit, hanging lamps violently swayed.

Bert McKay burst out with a hard string of profanity while Charley Barrett, nearest the front spindle-doors, poked his head out. "She's a-going," yelled Charley. "That one they tossed in from the busted doorway. Come look, you fellers, the walls are buckling."

Danvers and Gleeson sprang ahead. The four of them stepped forth onto Corbett's plankwalk and halted, turning stiff, turning stunned. Barrett was not entirely correct though; the jailhouse did not fall. But its walls extruded at a dangerous angle, its roofline was settling at the centre, and a big, diaphanous cloud of cordite and dust was rising up over the building.

Most of that roadway gunfire died out. A few snipers still threw lead into the ruined building but generally the attackers stood awed and simply watched, believing as Danvers and his men also believed, the building was going to collapse any moment now. When it did not, when it groaningly settled and shuddered but refused to buckle, men shouted back and forth across from it where most of the attackers seemed to be congregating, fully in view now, confident they were entirely safe because there was no gunfire coming back from Riley's jailhouse.

Some attackers even cheered or made derisive cat-calls towards the building, evidently firmly believing Gleeson and whomever had been defending the place with him, was still in there.

Bert McKay, stung by some of those taunting calls, dropped to one knee and raised his carbine. Gleeson said nothing, he simply dropped a hand to McKay's shoulder and powerfully squeezed. Barrett looked around and down and growled.

"Bert; you simpleton. You want 'em to turn an' see us up here? Let 'em storm the damned place; all they'll find is an empty jailhouse."

McKay lowered the Winchester but he neither rose up nor softened his wintry expression.

Danvers, standing there beside Gleeson, said quietly, "We can swing around through the alleyway and come in behind 'em, can't we, Phil?"

Gleeson nodded. He had had paralleling thoughts, but had abandoned them in favour of something much less spectacular but a whole lot safer. "Or we can get out of this damned town until morning, Bill, rest up, get some horses, and come riding back in when everyone's sober—wearing our badges. I think daylight may make a big difference in how these people feel—daylight and sobriety."

Gleeson was recalling something Jack Corbett had once said to him concerning Oliver Furth's influence in the Plume country.

Danvers stood lost in contemplative thought for a long time. What jerked him back to the present was a solitary loud gunshot as those attacking men began converging upon the hushed and ruined jailhouse, boldly walking forth into plain sight with mellow starshine running over them, each with a gun in hand, each grimly intent upon victory.

A long-legged man was in mid-stride when the gunshot sounded. He stopped, drew fully upright and started to turn, to face around looking back the way he'd just come. He did not complete the turn but crumpled quietly, folded over and went face down in the churned roadway.

Men wildly scattered crying warnings to other men. Some ran forward to flatten against the front jailhouse wall as though they believed that shot had come from within. Others, not considering where the shot had come from at all, simply fled as swiftly as they could run.

Bert McKay got up off his one knee slowly and stiffly. "Moe," he said, more to himself than to the others around him. "Dammit all, that was Moe got shot down out there. Charley; did you see his face when he turned and the moonlight struck it?"

"I saw," agreed Barrett. "Doggone it Bert, we been ridin' like maniacs near a year to do that—and now there's only Ralph left."

Danvers broke in to say, "Inside everybody. The way those men are scattering we might be recognized."

Back in Corbett's bar McKay and Barrett continued glum and disconsolate-looking. One of them said dryly to Gleeson: "Was that your friend again, Phil? Dammit; what's he tryin' to do—fight this whole danged fight all by himself?"

Gleeson shrugged. "He's narrowing the odds and that's all I care about." Gleeson watched Bannister for a moment, considered their straining captives over against the wall, beckoned Danvers over to the bar and walked in that direction while McKay and Barrett returned to the roadway doors to look out, to watch angry, apprehensive men darting uneasily here and there seeking good cover from that invisible marksman.

"What do you think?" Gleeson asked. "Want to ride out, let the town cool off, then ride back behind our badges?"

Danvers gingerly probed his side before he scowlingly replied to this. "We could," he said, tentatively agreeing. "What's on your mind, Phil?"

"Furth and Porter. I figure, when the liquor wears off with the others and they don't find us in the jailhouse, most of 'em will have had enough; will head for home. I'd like to be out at Furth's ranch when he and Porter and their Maple Leaf men ride in."

Danvers looked at his red fingertips, considered them a long time, then tiredly nodded. "All right. We'll need horses and a place for our prisoners though."

Gleeson nodded and swung to look over at Bannister.

FIFTEEN

CHET BANNISTER told Gleeson, in response to the deputy's inquiry, that if Gleeson and the others would help him with the prisoners as far as the liverybarn loft, he'd sit up there until the federal marshals returned to Plume, with his prisoners.

This problem settled, Gleeson rounded up Barrett and McKay, beckoned to Bill Danvers and led the entire party out through the back-alley exit of Corbett's saloon into the solid night.

They went northward as far as a side-road, swung west

and, being too far above the centre of all that yelling southward to be seen, hiked on across Plume's wide roadway as far as the second north-south alleyway. Here, they walked along to that spot where they'd been not more than half an hour earlier—the rear entrance to Banning's barn.

It was no problem getting their prisoners up into the loft. The cowboys seemed to have lost all will to resist when they discovered that there were four—not one—federal lawmen involved in this fight. They were, for the most part, thoroughly crestfallen. Those who might have offered some kind of a plea, found peering down the cocked barrel of Chet Bannister's Winchester disconcerting enough to keep them quite silent.

Downstairs in the barn's gloomy runway four horses were rigged out, four men mounted them and rode boldly out into the alleyway, wheeled northward and went loping on out of town. Behind them a few gunshots erupted irregularly, indicating to Gleeson that the attackers, no longer concerned with the wrecked jailhouse, were firing at shadows, perhaps even at each other, demoralized more by the invisible assassin among them than they had ever been by the defending gunfire from Riley's office.

The night was paler and brighter beyond town. It seemed full of promise too, and except for an occasional rough word from Bill Danvers whose side was fearfully painful under the jolting run of a livery animal, the spirits of those men rose steadily until, within gunshot-distance of Oliver Furth's Maple Leaf ranch, Charley Barrett said to Bert McKay: "I've changed my mind; I don't want to settle down on some dull damned farm after all."

They came slowly into the Maple Leaf yard, four abreast, Winchesters balanced across laps, heads up and eyes searching. They made only a small amount of noise passing the bunkhouse but it was enough to rouse the cook, a man of indeterminate but considerable years. He came to the doorway yawning and scratching his belly, clad inelegantly in nothing more decorous than soiled long underwear and a fretful, sleepy expression.

Those four men wheeled in facing forward, none speaking, none smiling, none making any move to dismount. The cook looked, stopped scratching, stopped yawning, and stood on without moving considering four worn, smudged faces and four sets of unwaveringly hard eyes.

"The bosses ain't here," he croaked, looking longest at big Bill Danvers, whose side was partially bare and blood-smudged.

Gleeson reached into a pocket, drew forth his badge and stoically pinned it upon his shirt-front. On either side of him the others also did this, still without speaking. The cook's eyes grew restless and frightened. He snapped his mouth closed and waited until Gleeson and Danvers had dismounted, carbines in hand, then he said swiftly, "I don't know nothin' about it—whatever it was. I been here all night and I can prove—"

"Shuddup!"

The cook went instantly silent. Gleeson stepped up onto the bunkhouse porch, reached forth, caught the cook roughly by a shoulder and flung him down towards Danvers, stuck his head inside the bunkhouse and gradually stiffened in the doorway. Eventually turning toward the others he said, "There's a shot man in here."

Danvers pushed the cook back. Barrett and McKay got down. The three of them herded the cook back inside where Gleeson was lighting a lamp, and into the shrieking silence a faint voice spoke up huskily from a wall bunk, saying, "All right, I'm through. My gun's hangin' at the foot of the bunk."

They crowded up to peer at the injured cowboy. He looked very pale even in that warm, orange lampglow. Danvers bent a little studying his face. He said, "Young feller, how did you get back here? That looks like quite a hole you've got in your chest."

"Couple of riders for a neighbouring outfit who'd had enough—who sobered up—brought me back."

Gleeson turned, saw the cook standing with his back to the westerly log wall, his face grey, and said, "Any more wounded ones around here?"

The cook vigorously shook his head. "No sir, deputy. No more of any kind have come back. That there's the only one."

"All the same," growled Danvers from beside the wounded man's bunk, "Charley, you and Bert have a good look around. If the cook's lying we'll yank up a wagon-tongue and hang him from it."

Barrett and McKay left the bunkhouse. Gleeson drew up a chair for Danvers, motioned the cook over where he could keep an eye on him, and leaned upon the wall.

To the injured rangerider Danvers said, "Give us the facts and don't hold anything back."

The cowboy began speaking. He told of delivering an

envelope of money to Sheriff Riley in town for Dewey Porter. He said this money was for standing the drinks at Banning's saloon, and it was also partial payment to the Morgan brothers for leading the assault against the jail.

Gleeson stood there listening to all this. The cowboy kept on talking for a full fifteen minutes. When he'd pause Danvers would roughly prod him. When it was all out in the open Danvers looked wryly up at Gleeson, his eyes like wet iron.

"It's enough, plus what the four of us went through tonight, to bring an awful lot of damned fools to trial on an assortment of charges ranging from obstructing justice to attempted murder."

Gleeson looked from Danvers to the wounded man. One thing was troubling him. "You've mentioned Oliver Furth only a couple of times," he said. "It's always been Dewey Porter. You got a grudge against Porter and have some idea of shielding Furth?"

The cowboy weakly shook his head. "It was Dewey from start to finish. All us riders knew that, deputy. Oliver Furth—sure, he wanted someone's heart for Dean's death—but it was Dewey who sent for the Morgans usin' Furth's name. It was Dewey set things up with Terry Riley in town too. I know that's how it was 'cause Dewey used me as his messenger a lot. He used all of us an' we figured the thing out."

"You didn't like it but you went right along with it," said Gleeson tartly.

The cowboy swung his glance off Gleeson, ran it around the room, found the terrified cook over against the wall and kept his troubled gaze upon him, turning sullen and bitter towards the federal lawmen.

Danvers rose up, winced, put a hand over his side and jerked his head as he started across to the bunkhouse doorway. When Gleeson joined him over there Danvers said in a low voice, "We've got more than enough to clinch the lot of them, Phil. Let's get into position for this Furth and his boys when they ride in." Danvers eased his shoulders back against the door-sill and faintly smiled. "I don't mind admitting I'm dang near used up. I'd like to sit down somewhere with m'carbine and just quietly wait."

Gleeson, until now unmindful of the marshal's probable weakness resulting from that lost blood, turned as Barrett and McKay returned.

"Nothing," said McKay. "The place is as empty of people as an abandoned mine-shaft."

Gleeson nodded. "Bert; help Bill over to the veranda of the main house. Fix him up with a chair at the veranda's north end and you stay over there with him. Charley; you and I'll take positions here inside the bunkhouse. Now listen, all of you, when those Maple Leaf men come ridin' in if there's any talkin' to be done I'll do it. I'd like them to believe I'm alone inside their bunkhouse, but whether they believe that or not, I don't want them to know Bert and Bill are behind them over at the main house. Time enough for them to find that out if they go for their guns. We beat 'em once by not being where we were supposed to be. I'd like to pull the same thing again if it's possible."

Danvers nodded, pushed off the wall and turned away. He and Bert started on across the yard. Gleeson watched until darkness over at Furth's residence effectively hid them from sight, then he said, "Charley; put our horses out back somewhere, then come on into the bunkhouse."

Barrett though, had been having some second thoughts. Instead of immediately obeying he said, "Phil; what about Ralph Morgan. He's still loose you know, and Bill said the Morgans were our first—"

"Charley, dammit all, if Ralph doesn't come back with Furth and Porter I'll buy you a new Stetson hat."

"A hat I don't need," retorted Barrett sharply. "What I'll need if Ralph gets away again is someone to ride him down with me."

"You've got my word on it," answered Gleeson. "Now take care of the horses and hurry back. Our friends could ride in here anytime within the next half hour or so."

Time dragged for Gleeson. His nerves were raw, his eyes felt as though sand were beneath the lids; they grated each time he moved them. For lack of anything better to do he bandaged the wounded cowboy's gaping chest-wound. The Maple Leaf cook watched this from his vantage point against the rear wall. Once he spoke out, saying, "I had nothin' to do with it, deputy. I been right here on the ranch all the blessed time."

Gleeson's sharp reply silenced the cook: "I got a little information for you, cookie," he said. "When you have knowledge of a crime which is to be committed and you make no attempt to get that knowledge to law officers, you're as guilty of the crime as the men are who commit it."

The cowboy watched Gleeson's experienced hands fashion that bandage. He said a little tremulously, "How about it, deputy; will I make it or not?"

Gleeson completed the bandage, straightened up and said, "You'll make it all right. You'll probably be the healthiest prisoner in the territorial prison and maybe, when you get out again, you'll be a heap wiser too. You know, feller, the world is full of damned fools—but in my book the biggest damned fool is the one who lets himself be badgered into something."

The cowboy weakly inclined his head and tried to make a little smile. "Yeah; especially against fellers who can shoot as straight as you fellers can. Deputy; not a one of us had any notion you weren't alone in that jailhouse until all those shotguns started goin' off. An' I'll tell you somethin' else too—until the four of you walked through that door wearin' your badges, I had no idea there was so many lawmen in the country."

Gleeson picked up a tobacco sack lying beside the injured man. He worked up a cigarette, lit it and popped it between the rider's ashen lips. "You're luckier'n some of your friends, feller. Some of them will never know who they were up against. Tell me something; how long has Sheriff Riley been on Furth's payroll?"

"Not Furth, deputy, on Dewey Porter's payroll. Dewey promised Riley three sections of Maple Leaf land to start a cow outfit on—when Dewey got control of Maple Leaf."

Gleeson made himself a smoke, lit it and blew smoke downward. "You could've told Furth," he murmured. "You were takin' his pay; you owed him some loyalty."

The cowboy removed his cigarette and looked steadily at it. "Yeah, I could've," he said. "Only—Dewey promised each of us as helped him the same amount of deeded land when he got control of Maple Leaf."

"Busy boy," said Gleeson in the same dry, quiet tone. "Dewey was a very busy boy."

Charley Barrett thrust his head inside from the bunkhouse porch. "Riders comin'," he called softly.

Gleeson looked at the cowboy, at the cook, and warningly wagged his head. "Call out, either one of you, and I'll promise you the first slug—right through the guts."

He walked out where Barrett was standing with his cradled Winchester listening to the faint but discernible sound of horsemen rushing northward through the night. Barrett looked around. "Hear 'em?" he asked.

Gleeson nodded. He heard them; they were coming on at a swift gait, but the longer Gleeson listened the less it sounded as though this could be all that remained of Oliver Furth's men. He went to the edge of the little porch, stood stock-still and cocked his head. It didn't sound like more than a pair of riders, three or four at the most. He lifted his voice to softly call over toward the main house.

"Careful; this doesn't sound right. Don't shoot until I do."

Barrett swept up and leaned there, also listening. "Sounds right to me," he said. "Who else could it be? Furth or his rangeboss is all."

Gleeson made an impatient gesture for silence. Charley closed his mouth but he scowled as he listened.

The sound swept steadily closer. There was no other noise in the roundabout night until a horse nickered somewhere behind the barn and Barrett swore over this.

Gleeson said, "It's all right, Charley; the way those men are riding they couldn't hear it anyway."

SIXTEEN

WHEN THOSE INVISIBLE RIDERS were a hundred yards out they slowed to a fast walk. Once they halted as though not quite sure what lay ahead, then resumed their steady approach. By that time every listening man at the Maple Leaf had counted the separate sounds and had come up with the same number—three horsemen.

Gleeson put aside his Winchester, drew his handgun and stepped off the bunkhouse porch to pace ahead a little distance and stand quiet in thick shadows by a shed of some kind.

Maple Leaf's yard was utterly still. Charley Barrett had killed the light at the bunkhouse and was standing over there to one side of the open door with a carbine.

The riders came on in single file, like a small band of Indians, one behind the other. Gleeson, seeing the heavy cut of a man's broad shoulders against the paler sky raised his gun. That first rider had a rifle across his lap but the others seemed to lack this indication of hostility or wariness. A hundred feet out that first rider drew rein again, he seemed to be sniffing the night, gauging it in response to some instinctive warning. That was when Gleeson deliberately cocked his pistol.

At this unmistakable sound the first man turned stiff, swung his head in the direction of that sharp, threatening noise, and Gleeson sighted his fiercely up-curling dragoon moustache.

"Corbett you damned fool," he softly called. "You came within an ace of getting it this time."

The mounted man cocked his head. When he spoke his voice was not the least disturbed, but it was sharp and truculent. "Is that you Gleeson? Step out where a man can see you."

Gleeson complied, moving slowly onward and at the same time lowering his sixgun. "Who's with you, Corbett?"

"Couple of ladies; allies of yours but I'm not so sure they're your friends."

Corbett eased over, swung down and came to rest beside his horse. He made sure it was Gleeson walking over, then turned his head and barked for those riders behind him to dismount. They did so; April Bannister and Mary Bonneville. They led their horses up closer to Corbett and halted, peering ahead where Gleeson was approaching. Corbett reached up, shoved his saddle-gun into its boot and turned forward again as Gleeson halted ten feet off.

"There's sure hell to pay in town," related the saloonman. "Everybody was plumb certain you and whoever was in the jailhouse with you got killed. Then when they stormed the place it was empty." Corbett's large teeth shone in the night. "Now, them as are still fired up, are going all over the place peering into henhouses and cellars and my saloon tryin' to find you."

"Porter?" asked Gleeson. "Porter and Furth and a lanky feller named Ralph Morgan?"

"And a few others. Everybody is sure uneasy though.

The word's been spreading that there are a bunch more U.S. marshals with you. I'm not exactly certain all those men who're lookin' for you want to kill you; I got a notion some of them just want to make their peace with the law."

Charley Barrett strolled up from the direction of the bunkhouse. Easterly, also walking slowly, Bert McKay appeared, carbine in hand, sure from the sound of those voices there was to be no trouble, yet not willing to completely drop his guard either.

"Tell me something," queried Gleeson. "Was that you shooting into them from behind?"

"Yup. I downed my share of 'em."

"Where were you?"

Corbett grinned. "Here and there, deputy. I been in that town seven years; in that time a man gets to know where the vantage points are. By the way, have you any idea who a couple of those men were I shot?"

"Yeah," said Charley Barrett dryly. "The Morgans. My pardner and I've been trailing them a year tryin' to get just one decent sighting. We never made it, but in one night a feller doin' a little random-shootin' downs two of 'em off-hand." Barrett wagged his head.

McKay stopped a few feet off and said, "How about this Maple Leaf outfit; are they comin' out here?"

Corbett nodded. "They are. I heard Porter tell Furth they'd have to come back here for ammunition and fresh horses. That's when I brought the ladies and high-tailed it for this place."

"Why?" asked McKay. "Why here? Hell—I mean heck—if that outfit's comin' you'd be pretty bad off— just you against all those others."

Corbett looked steadily at McKay for a time and Gleeson saw his expression roughening in the face of Bert's suspicion. But when Corbett answered he showed none of his annoyance.

"We came out here without any intention of staying, deputy. We rode hard to get here first, turn all the Maple Leaf horses loose, and hunt for Porter's ammunition cache and destroy that too. Then we aimed to keep right on going so we wouldn't be caught." Corbett swung back to face Gleeson now. "We had another idea too; we thought, since you obviously weren't in town, Gleeson, you just might have some similar idea and be out here too."

Gleeson nodded, turned to McKay and said, "How's Bill?"

"Worn out and weak but otherwise all right."

"Go on back, Bert. Stay with him. Charley and I'll take care of Corbett and the ladies."

McKay turned and trudged back the way he had come. Charley Barrett moved ahead to reach for the reins of those three horses. He smiled at April and Mary Bonneville as he started barnward with the animals.

Gleeson stepped around Corbett, saw April first and said, "You all right, Missus Bannister?"

"I'm all right, deputy. Where is my husband?"

"Safe, I think. He's guarding a dozen prisoners we took back in town."

"Is he all right?"

Gleeson considered that immature, troubled face and sardonically smiled. "As all right as a man can be who's been threatened, shot at, bombed and scairt out of a year's growth, all in the same night, ma'm."

He stepped over to Mary Bonneville. The tall, handsome woman contrasted strongly with the shorter and younger girl. She seemed unruffled and except for a heavy curl of dark hair lying out of place across her forehead, stood there as distant, as unapproachable as she had been the first time Gleeson had met her.

" 'You all right?" Gleeson asked.

Mary inclined her head. "Are you?"

"Bright-eyed and bushy-tailed," he said. "You know; when we met before and you gave me that little gun—I forgot something."

"I know," murmured Mary, giving Gleeson look for look. "That worried me too. Until the fighting started in town I half believed you couldn't be much of a lawman to overlook something as important as that."

"As what?" challenged Gleeson.

"As important as determining how I came to have Dean Furth's pistol."

Gleeson nodded, stood there gazing upon that lovely woman saying nothing for a while. "Where did you get the thing?" he eventually said.

"Dewey Porter walked out of the saloon after Bannister had been led away by Terry Riley, pushed the gun under the plankwalk and got on his horse and rode out of town."

"And you saw him do all this, retrieved the gun and kept it?"

Mary nodded. Her eyes showed a veiled interest in Gleeson. Gently putting her head a little to one side she said, "How did you come to forget asking me

138

that, deputy?"

"Would you really like to know, ma'm?"

"Yes."

"Well; it was this way. I never in my whole life saw a woman who affected me as you did—and I just plain forgot all about it."

Jack Corbett broadly smiled, thinking Gleeson was deliberately saying this to break the composure of Mary Bonneville's unchanging expression. Then he saw that this was not so at all; that Gleeson was dead-serious.

April Bannister moved close and gouged Corbett pitilessly with a thumb. "Stare, you idiot," she hissed at the saloonman, shoved Corbett and kept shoving until the pair of them were over near the bunkhouse where Charley Barrett was just coming up after having stabled the horses.

Gleeson knew those two had moved off. He also knew that standing exposed in that faint-lighted yard was not the wisest thing he had ever done, but until Mary spoke again he didn't care.

"Maybe you wondered why I rode into town knowing trouble was imminent, after telling you I didn't want to become involved."

"Well," Gleeson candidly answered, "I was surprised to see you walk out of Corbett's bar; but too many other things were hanging fire right then for me to wonder much about anything."

"But would you be interested in knowing why I rode in, deputy?"

"Yes'm, I would."

"Because I was worried about you."

Gleeson felt colour rising in his face. He knew he should now say something gallant, but could not for the life of him think of anything that even came close, so he said nothing.

"I didn't know you had friends. I thought you were bracing the town, Dewey Porter and Oliver Furth, all by yourself. I wanted to ask you not to try it. That's why I walked out of the saloon when you ordered me back inside."

"I thank you for your interest," said Gleeson, and took Mary Bonneville's arm, turned and slow-paced with her onward toward the bunkhouse. "I couldn't tell you about the U.S. Marshal and two more deputies being in Plume. I couldn't even risk telling Corbett. Later on of course I could have, but by then all hell had busted loose and I never had the chance."

Mary murmured: "I understand. We all understand. On the ride out here we pieced it all together. I'd like to meet the others. You are a different breed of men than I'm used to, deputy. It's been a long time since Plume had your kind. I think my father was the last of them."

Gleeson stopped, half turned and said quietly, "Maybe, when this is all over and I get time to clean up a little, we could have supper and talk about it."

Mary smiled; it made her seem girlish and sweet and warm. "I'd like that, deputy."

"Ma'm, the name is Phil."

"I'd like that, Phil."

As they stood close in the night Charley called softly to Gleeson saying, "Phil; that cowboy's wound is bleedin' again." This broke the mood and Gleeson turned, resenting both Charley and the injured cowboy in the bunkhouse. He and Mary paced along to where the others were standing upon the bunkhouse porch. There, Mary and April left to go inside and re-bandage the injured man, while Gleeson and Corbett and Charley Barrett stood in the soft night each occupied with his own thoughts.

After a while Jack Corbett, leaning back so that the overhang obscured his features, said, "Gleeson; like I told you—you comin' to town sparked bad trouble. But I wasn't altogether right about the consequences. I thought sure Bannister was going to get lynched. I reckon I owe you sort of an apology."

Charley Barrett found a rickety chair, eased down upon it and this made a scraping sound, the only noise anywhere around until Gleeson answered Corbett.

"The trouble was coming anyway, Corbett. Whenever I ride into a town it's because there's trouble. My job is to somehow steer the trouble into channels that get it over with before it gets plumb out of hand and a lot of folks are hurt by it. The trouble is, things don't always work out the way they should."

"Yeah. You're talkin' about Oliver Furth, aren't you?"

"Furth and others. A lot of men were made fools of tonight. Some of them died, some of them sobered up and got a good look at themselves and what they were doing. We took twelve in that last category tonight. Bannister's guarding them back in town. Sometimes I feel pity for men like those, but I never feel any pity for men like Dewey Porter."

"How about Oliver Furth?"

Gleeson turned, listened to the stillness for a moment before answering this, heard nothing and turned back. "Furth's got an excuse—his dead son—but an excuse doesn't change anything, Corbett. Furth couldn't have avoided knowing part of what's been going on. Maybe he didn't know Porter's real scheme, but the part of it he did know about was just as bad. Furth wanted Bannister killed. I tried to tell him his son wasn't murdered; he wouldn't even listen." Gleeson paused again; this was not an easy thing to explain.

"Sure, Furth had his personal agony; I'm not able to say how I'd react under the same conditions. But I can say that Furth has his share of the guilt, and the law says he'll have to pay for that."

Corbett made a long, soft sigh. He looked out into the paling night saying nothing for a while, but eventually gently nodded his head up and down.

"You're a fair man, deputy," he ultimately murmured. "You've pegged Furth just right and you don't even know the man. But I'm different from you in one way— I can feel sorry for him."

"I didn't say I don't feel sorry for the man," said Gleeson. "What I'm saying now is that, pity aside, he's let anguish and the wish for revenge blind him, and now he's going to pay for that."

SEVENTEEN

TIME SEEMED TO DRAG BY to those people at the Maple Leaf who had earlier experienced so much capsuled into so short a period of living moments.

Mary Bonneville came out where the men were, upon the bunkhouse porch. April Bannister remained inside and the cook was making coffee on a little heating-stove inside which gave off a fine aroma.

Over at the main ranch house there was not a sound where Bill Danvers and Bert McKay were, but off behind the house a setting, sickle moon was growing steadily more yellow, more faint-lighted and fading.

Charley Barrett arose to offer his chair to Mary Bonneville. She thanked him but passed on to where Gleeson was leaning, stopped and drew in a big breath, slowly let it out and glanced at the fading heavens.

"It is so peaceful now," she murmured to Gleeson. "So serene and quiet."

He nodded. "The world is a place of contrasts." He started to face around, to admire the sweep of her flawless throat. Charley Barrett broke in to solidly say something.

"Riders coming Phil."

Mary's head came down and around. Gleeson also turned southward. Across the yard others had heard that faint-distant drumming too; Bill Danvers called forth in his deep-booming way: "Heads up over there. Phil—Charley—look careful."

This was an unnecessary admonition, but it brought Chet Bannister's wife to the bunkhouse doorway where she stood solemnly listening, solemnly considering the others.

It sounded to Gleeson that this party of riders was coming on in considerable force. Charley Barrett, evidently with similar thoughts, said, "At least ten of them and maybe more." He said this as though eliciting comment from Gleeson, but nothing came back to him.

Gleeson went over, retrieved his Winchester and returned. He jerked his head at April Bannister in the doorway. "Get inside," he ordered. "You too, Mary. Bar the door from the inside and don't open it unless one of us tells you to."

Mary hesitated long enough to look deep into Gleeson's eyes. Then she wordlessly turned away, passed into the little building and immediately closed the door.

Barrett stepped up even with Gleeson. He had a dead cigarette between his lips. When he spoke this thing bobbed erratically up and down.

"You better not let 'em get too far into the yard," he warned. "If there's fightin' an' they get among all these sheds we're not goin' to be in too good a position, Phil."

The horsemen did not slacken off as Gleeson half thought they might, but kept on loping steadily northward. He levered his carbine, peered in, closed the slide and stood on, one thumb over the hammer, one finger curled on the trigger. All the lassitude of this past quiet hour worked on him; it was a struggle coming alert again, dredging up his former wariness and temper. He did not like the idea of those women behind him in the bunkhouse, but Jack Corbett's presence ameliorated this feeling somewhat. Corbett was a tough man.

Suddenly those riders stopped down the night beyond sight of the watchers. One moment they were loping along, the next moment they were not, and there was no

144

sound from them. This inexplicable occurrence struck down through Gleeson bringing on a quick wariness. He turned, saw Barrett's face wreath into an uneasy frown, and saw Corbett beyond slowly come erect and straining.

Corbett whispered: "Furth's a careful man. Maybe they suspicion something or maybe they're just naturally careful. In either case it adds up to the same thing; they're sending someone ahead to scout the yard."

Gleeson privately agreed with this. "Back," he hissed. "Back out of sight and stay still." He saw those two beside him fade off the porch and around the bunkhouse wall northward. He glided southward and stepped down over there, moved along the bunkhouse wall to its rear turning, and there blended into the darker gloom round back.

A man's complaining voice came mutedly from out where those horsemen had halted. If he was answered Gleeson did not hear it. He made it across a moonlighted empty space and immediately thereafter got back into darkness where a blacksmith-shop stood, sooty and strong-smelling of forge fires. Here he waited a long time not moving and scarcely even breathing. If Porter and Furth had indeed sent someone on ahead afoot, he would have to pass around into the southward yard beyond the smithy. When he did this Gleeson would see him for the elemental reason that there was no other building to obstruct the southward view.

It was a long, tense wait, but Gleeson saw him. The man was lanky and quiet-moving. He made no sound and yet Gleeson got the impression from the way this scout was walking that he personally believed this scouting business a total waste of time.

The man didn't try for cover until he was east of the same building which shielded Gleeson, then he swung to his right and came on with long, thrusting strides.

Gleeson drew his handgun, stepped to the south corner of his shed, raised the gun and hung there. His enemy would come around the shed unless he changed course, which he did not do, but once he halted, twisted and gazed over at the main house as though he'd heard something. Gleeson's heart sloshed around in its cavernous place sounding very loud to Gleeson in all that hush.

The cowboy straightened up and came on again, still moving with a kind of careless unconcern, both arms swinging, both long legs rising and falling. When he was close enough for Gleeson to hear abrasive, tiny sound of bootsoles over flinty earth, the cowboy suddenly halted. Gleeson heard the quick, abrupt rush of the man's indrawn breath. Until that moment it had not occurred to Gleeson to look earthward. Now he did—and saw an image of his own outline with upraised pistol, projected outward from beyond the smithy in a tell-tale shadow.

He had no time for thought; his reaction to discovery was swift and bold. He leapt out and brought his pistol downward in a long sweep. But the cowboy was also moving; he had his gun swinging free of leather when Gleeson appeared. He fired. That bullet laid its lethal breath against Gleeson's cheek and sped on past.

Gleeson spun sideways to present a thin target and avoided a second bullet in this fashion, then his gun lanced a crimson slash into the gloom. The Maple Leaf man was spun completely around by impact. He fell into the shed with a solid sound, slid downward and sat there, looking incredulous, looking speechless, waiting for the killing shot. It never came. Gleeson let his gun hang. He stepped over, knelt and hurled the cowboy's handgun far out behind him, squared the man's shoulders against the shed-wall and searched for the wound. It was a bad one; in at the navel and out alongside the spinal column. The cowboy though, appeared to be in no pain, although his astonished look did not depart and he kept staring over at Gleeson. Finally he managed a few words.

"Hell; so this is where you went. I never would've figured it."

" 'Better just rest easy," said Gleeson, twisting as a man's alarmed cry rang in from southward. "Too bad you fired, pardner. Too bad for you and too bad for my friends an' me. We were waiting. I reckon now the surprise is done for."

It was; Gleeson heard horsemen milling out in the southward night, heard them calling back and forth, then break out in a hard charge down toward the yard. It did not occur to Gleeson at that moment this charge had been ordered by Dewey Porter and Ralph Morgan against what those men thought was no more than a couple of men, which was what that calling back and forth had been about. Gleeson thought only of his exposed position, whirled upright and dashed back around the blacksmith shop, flattened there a moment to make certain his retreat was clear as far as the bunkhouse, then raced hard for that building.

He was half way across the intervening distance when those running horses appeared out of the darkness coming on fast. He saw in an instant he could not make it to the bunkhouse and threw himself belly-down in the dust.

One rider, catching sight of blurred movement, spun away in a sharp swoop towards Gleeson. He had his sixgun out and swinging. Gleeson looked up, saw this man bearing down and frantically rolled. A bullet struck where he had been causing an eruption of dun-dust. Gleeson got off a shot of his own, rolled again and gathered both legs under him. The cowboy yanked his animal around, fired a snap-shot, missed and tried hard to run Gleeson down. This was a mistake for Gleeson was no longer helplessly prone. He dropped his pistol, steadied himself and when the horse's shoulder brushed him Gleeson sprang, was near-blinded by a red burst of gunfire, closed his fingers over the rider's upper leg and threw himself violently backwards. The cowboy let off a high yell as he went drunkenly sideways off his frightened horse. He grasped at the horse's mane, missed and fell like stone. Gleeson stumbled over the man's legs, fought for balance, whirled and threw himself across his adversary.

The cowboy was a tall, lank man and ordinarily would have employed his wiriness to spring away. Now though, that stunning fall had hurt him. He tried rolling clear, tried kicking out at his enemy, but each movement was sluggish. Gleeson reared back, chopped a fierce blow downward, and the cowboy shuddered his full length, dropped his head against the earth and thickly moaned. Gleeson got off, caught the man roughly and yanked him upright. The cowboy's feet would not track and his legs seemed made of putty. He hung in Gleeson's grip slowly, wetly, blinking, not quite unconscious but on the verge of it.

Elsewhere those charging riders raced down into Maple Leaf's yard all in a wild charge. Their guns flashed in the gloom swinging left and right, their cries made the hair stiffen at the base of Gleeson's skull. He saw them split up and go phantom-like toward the main house and that smaller log building where Barrett, Corbett, and the two women were, firing and yelling. It seemed to Gleeson, pushing his prisoner roughly along, holding his prisoner's sixgun in his own fist, that Porter's riders had reason to be this bold; so far only one gunshot had blasted outward at them. That shot had come from the bunkhouse.

He knew Bill Danvers though; knew instinctively what the U.S. Marshal was waiting for. Knew also that Danvers was making McKay also hold off until every one of those riders was well into the yard and well in view. Then the bracketing shots came, tearing into the night adding their fierce and lethal symphony to the other savage sounds. Danvers and McKay had caught the Maple Leaf men from behind. They levered and fired and levered to fire again. It seemed to Gleeson there had to be at least ten men over there at the main house for all those gunshots although he knew there could not possibly be more than two men.

The bunkhouse too finally poured a murderous fire into the mounted men. Jack Corbett and Charley Barrett were inside, evidently; to Gleeson their shots sounded inordinately loud, as though coming from within four confining walls where trapped echoes beat upon one another increasing the noise.

A horseman who caught sight of Gleeson pushing his staggering captive along, hung up there staring, his handgun poised, his face contorted. This interlude, which could not have lasted more than a second at the most, seemed to Gleeson to endure half a lifetime. Out of the deafening tumult a bullet came, struck the mounted man head-on, made a meaty sound under impact, and the man's twisted face instantly altered to a look of speechless astonishment. He dropped his gun, turned loose all over and fell straight down without throwing out either hand to break the fall. His horse shied away, flung up its head and ran off northward into the night.

Gleeson recognized Dewey Porter in the crush of confused, straining horses and men. He threw up the gun in his fist, but Porter faded out in the mêlée, only his recognizable voice shouting into the tumult.

"Break off! Ride north! *Get out of this yard!*"

A horse and rider went down in a threshing heap fifty feet ahead of Gleeson. The rider, pinned by one leg, flung himself one way and another. He cried out for aid, for his companions to free him. None heeded this man's screams at all. It was every man for himself now; riders were plunging clear of that straining mass of men and animals, whipping around to get away from the deadly cross-fire between main house and bunkhouse.

Gleeson saw two men make it. Both lunged out northward riding far forward over the necks of their panicked mounts. Most of that decimated band though thought only of getting down, getting away from the skylined

height of a saddle. They hit the ground running, sometimes shooting but generally concentrating only upon
flight to some kind of protective shelter among the buildings. A few made it but not many; four injured men lay
moaning in the smoke and dust choked yard, feebly
moving. Two, one of whom was that mounted man
Gleeson had seen so clearly in front of the bunkhouse,
lay flat and entirely still, face-down-dead.

Gleeson came even with the pinned man, heeded his
cries for succour, kicked this man's pistol away with his
foot, caught him by the shoulders and got him free. The
man fainted in Gleeson's arms. He saw this, prepared to
drop him and cross the last twenty feet to the
bunkhouse's safety, when Jack Corbett ran up, wordlessly scooped up that man, turned and ran back to the
bunkhouse with him. Gleeson followed with his other
prisoner.

The gunfire was turning brisk again but there seemed
now to be no odds favouring either side, unless it was the
solid protection the lawmen had and which the Maple
Leaf riders did not have.

EIGHTEEN

G LEESON WAS ADMITTED to the bunkhouse by
Mary Bonneville who immediately slammed
and barred the door after him. It was pitch dark
in the little log bunkhouse with a choking atmosphere
made foul by gun-powder. The deafening sounds inside
that room drove Gleeson toward the rear wall.

One of those unpredictable interludes came; for a

while not a single gunshot was heard. The longer this interlude ran on the less it appeared that either side wished to break it. But the tension heightened throughout this period making men's nerves crawl.

Someone inside struck a guarded match, held it up behind a hat and said bleakly, "Phil; you got him." This was Charley Barrett.

"Got who, Charley?"

"Dammit, don't you recognize him? You captured Ralph Morgan."

Gleeson had not recognized the man he'd dragged off the horse; had not in fact had a free moment to even speculate on the identity of his prisoner. Now he turned, peered over where that dying small flame shone against slack, waxen features, and recognized the notorious outlaw from pictures he'd seen of him on wanted posters. But Gleeson's concern over this was considerably less than was Charley Barrett's.

"For now never mind that," he told Barrett, whose match flickered out plunging the bunkhouse back into darkness again. "Tie his arms behind him."

Gleeson stepped over where Jack Corbett and April Bannister were bending over the unconscious man Corbett had brought in. April looked up at Gleeson.

"His leg is crushed. He must have fainted."

Gleeson said unsympathetically, "Yeah. I had to yank pretty hard to get him free of his horse. He passed out when I was pulling him loose." He touched Corbett's shoulder. "Leave him to the women," he said, straightening up. "It's too quiet out there."

The pair of them stepped over to the door, eased it

open a crack and peered out. Off in the brightening east where dawn was tinting an otherwise murky sky with its spreading blue-grey banners, fresh new light was coming onward and downward. Sunrise was not far off. Maple Leaf's littered, dusty yard was softly visible and that peculiar, unnatural depth of lethal silence ran on making the pre-dawn world appear to be a stark and deadly place.

Corbett's hand closed vice-like around Gleeson's wrist. "Look," breathed the saloonman. "Yonder by the main house."

Gleeson swung his head, saw the outline of several men break clear of the darker background against Oliver Furth's residence moving ahead into the open yard. At his side Jack Corbett gently brought up his sixgun.

Gleeson frowned at this. "Hold it," he murmured, not certain yet about the identity of those men, but almost sure from the limp one of them was big Bill Danvers. "Hold it, Jack; I think it's all right."

There were four of those men across the yard. Two had their hands behind their heads. Behind these two came the second brace of men. It was one of these, not clearly visible yet, which seemed to Gleeson to be Bill Danvers.

Charley Barrett came pushing up, finished securing Ralph Morgan with ropes. Behind Charley Mary Bonneville and April Bannister stood on tiptoe also trying to make out those oncoming men.

Gleeson let off a long breath. "It's Danvers back there. Danvers and Bert McKay."

Barrett echoed this. Then he said, "They tryin' to get killed or something? Hell—" Barrett got no further.

Gleeson ahead of him in the doorway, suddenly unwound in a flash of movement. He had sighted something off in the steely north the others had not seen; a man stepped clear of an out-building. He stared hard down the yard where Danvers and McKay were herding their captives. Gleeson saw this lank stranger throw up a carbine and snug it back into his shoulder. He slammed back the bunkhouse door, jumped outside and fired from the hip. His shot did not score but it caused the sighting rifleman to wince, to miss with his own gunshot.

Out in the yard and half way across it Danvers, McKay and their two captives dropped like stone as that carbine slug sang high overhead.

Gleeson shot a second time and this time he was not moving. That distant rifleman wilted, took one backward step, levered his carbine and fired off a round. The bullet struck six feet from the bunkhouse into a log wall. Gleeson fired his third shot and the rifleman fell, dropped his carbine, raised up strainingly on all fours, teetered there, then finally collapsed under a hail of lead from Danvers and McKay out in the yard, Corbett and Barrett over at the bunkhouse.

Gleeson moved down off the porch before the last echoes faded out. He re-loaded as he crossed to that prone figure, toed the man over onto his back, stared for a hushed moment, then swung away heading for Danvers and McKay. His stride was angry. When he got up to the others he said fiercely: "Bill; what's the matter with you anyway—walkin' out into the yard like that?"

Danvers turned aside, spat, and turned back. He jerked an indignant thumb toward the two frozen-faced captives. "They said they were the only two left."

Gleeson put up his gun, wagged his head and said no more. The five of them continued on to the bunkhouse porch where Barrett, Corbett, and both girls were waiting.

Barrett, as soon as he saw McKay, said jubilantly "We got the last o' the Morgans, Bert. Got Ralph Morgan tied to a bunk inside."

"Alive?" said McKay, stopping at the porch steps.

Barrett nodded and broadly grinned.

Danvers went over to the porch edge, eased down there and looked upwards. "Anyone hurt?" he asked Gleeson, got back a dour head-shake and put up his gun, ran a dirty hand over his face and said, "Who was that damned sniper over yonder with the Winchester?"

"Dewey Porter," replied Gleeson.

"Is he dead?"

Gleeson nodded. He swung to gaze at their prisoners. "One more to hunt down yet," he muttered.

But Danvers and McKay both started shaking their heads. "If you're talkin' about Oliver Furth," said the U.S. Marshal, "you can forget it. He was one of the men killed in the roadway back in Plume." Danvers waved a careless hand at the two men he and McKay had taken prisoner. "Ask those two; that's why they surrendered. They figured with Furth dead in town and the rest of the Maple Leaf crew whipped here in the ranchyard, their interest in the battle was ended."

Gleeson, studying the faces of those two dull-looking, exhausted prisoners, felt rather than saw that this was the truth. He thought of something tart to say to the brace of

155

surrendered men but he did not say it, instead he went over where Charley Barrett was making a cigarette, held out his hand without saying anything, and Charley obligingly handed over both sack and papers. The two of them lit off the same match, inhaled, exhaled, and leaned there against the bunkhouse wall.

Mary Bonneville returned inside the battered bunkhouse. April followed her. Gleeson heard them at the little stove. He swung his head as McKay brought out Ralph Morgan, still with both arms firmly lashed behind his back, and the Maple Leaf's cook. To Morgan he said, "When did Furth get it?"

Morgan, a saturnine-looking, evil man, put his sullen stare upon Gleeson and did not speak. Out of the gloom behind him came Jack Corbett's business-like fist; it stopped just short of Morgan's face. The outlaw looked down, looked back along that thick arm to the fiercely moustached face behind it, and spoke up.

"Dunno who shot him; it was after we stormed the jailhouse an' found you fellers gone. The lot of us was walkin' back out into the roadway. Hell; there'd been a lousy sniper sneakin' around amongst us all night. Anyway; there was a gunshot. Furth grabbed his chest an' fell down. He was drilled straight through the brisket, deader'n a cussed post."

Beyond the renegade Jack Corbett's eyes gradually widened. He and Gleeson exchanged a long look, then Corbett gently raised his shoulders and let them fall; he could not have shot Oliver Furth because he was at the Maple Leaf when Furth was killed. He was plainly puzzled as to who had shot the rancher.

Gleeson saw this and said, in a way which only Corbett thoroughly understood. "It doesn't really matter. I heard it said once in town Furth had his share of enemies—that he couldn't influence everyone. I reckon one of those folks shot him. We'll probably never know who did it."

"Nor care," muttered Bill Danvers, pushing himself up off the porch, closing this particular topic with a careless gesture of one hand. "Say; are there any clean shirts in that bunkhouse?"

No one answered this right away. Not until the cook began to vigorously nod his head up and down. "Sure, Marshal, plenty of 'em. Want me to fetch you one?"

Danvers looked up at the cook, his expression sardonic. "Yeah; but that buys you nothin'," he growled, and swung towards Gleeson as the cook ducked inside. "Let's go," he said in the same growling tone. "Get the horses, tie the dead over their saddles, lash the prisoners astride and let's ride back through Plume."

They did this, but not until Mary and April came out with hot black coffee and every man there drank a cup full. It made a difference in each of them, that coffee. Even Danvers seemed imbued with new life, new vigour. He rode all the way back to Plume without a murmur, as though his injured side was no longer hurting him.

It was a savage-looking cavalcade that entered the little cowtown from the north with Phil Gleeson and U.S. Marshal Bill Danvers out front. Every lawman had his badge showing, every prisoner was tied and stiff in the saddle. The dead gently swayed with each slow step of their horses and none of those men, dead or living, looked any other way in the shocked eyes of the

157

townsmen who came forth to silently stare, than bitter and grim.

Chet Bannister came forth from the liverybarn with four armed townsmen helping him herd along his grey-faced prisoners. He fell in behind the column with April riding close to him, trudged along with the others as far as Terry Riley's wrecked jailhouse, and halted there when the others also halted.

Danvers got down last. He looked into the sombre faces that came quietly along from both plankwalks to stop and stare. He said: "Take a good look, folks. You probably knew some of these dead men. You've got some other dead men around here somewhere—Riley, your crooked sheriff, Oliver Furth, your biggest local cowman, and others I don't know—but who I saw die in your lousy roadway last night. Take a good long look—not just at the dead and the injured—but at yourselves as well. I'm only sorry I can't take the whole lot of you along for trial. I'd like to do that. There are some of you standing around here right now lookin' innocent who were in on the fightin' last night. You wanted to hang a man for murder. Well; let me tell you something: *Bannister didn't murder Dean Furth.* That was a fair fight and I can prove it." Danvers paused, turning in the soft morning light to look balefully at those blank, grey faces crowding around.

"That was a fair fight; Furth had a gun and he tried to use it. He just wasn't good enough or honest enough to make it a fair fight—and he died. One more thing, folks; maybe most of you learned something here last night. Those of you who didn't, let me tell you this: If I ever have to come here again, the good Lord help you. Don't ever try takin' the law into your own hands again. If you think you've got trouble, wire me—the U.S. Marshal—and I'll send someone to look into things, but don't you ever try it again."

Danvers turned, surveyed the wrecked jailhouse, saw Phil Gleeson watching him and made a wry face. "Take over," he said to Gleeson. "And if they've got a doctor in this sink-hole of a town send him over to my room at the hotel." Danvers tossed his reins to Charley Barrett, started to turn, halted, looked again at Gleeson and said, "Send me up a bottle of whisky too, Phil." He then pushed away and started across the roadway. People dropped back before him making a pathway.

Jack Corbett eased over next to Gleeson. "The whisky part of it is in my field, deputy. You can forget about that, I'll take it to him myself."

Gleeson nodded, put out a hand to detain Corbett, smiled at him and said, simply: "Thanks, Jack. If you ever get tired of pushing liquor over a bar, just let me know."

Corbett grinned, nodded, and also started away.

The crowd stirred, looking uneasy; some of the men began to drift away. Charley Barrett and Bert McKay said to Gleeson, almost simultaneously: "What'll we do with this herd of prisoners?"

Bannister pushed away from April's side. "I've got just the place," he volunteered. "I'll show you."

Gleeson nodded at Barrett and Bert McKay but he did not speak. He was tired and wrung-out. As those three rounded up their prisoners and started up the road northward with them, Gleeson's glance fell upon Mary Bonneville. It puzzled him how anyone who had been through so much could still manage to appear so unperturbed and clean. Mary saw this look and gravely smiled across at him. Gleeson finally moved; he went over to her, took her arm and as they moved away he said, "Let's substitute breakfast for that supper-date. I'm hungry enough to eat a horse, saddle and all."

Around them the people of Plume went quietly away from Terry Riley's sagging, bullet-marked, shell-battered jailhouse, good sunlight swept in over the town and softened, mellowed the dark stains of violence, bringing on a new day and a fresh opportunity for all the survivors of a long night of terror.

Center Point Publishing
600 Brooks Road • PO Box 1
Thorndike ME 04986-0001 USA

(207) 568-3717

US & Canada:
1 800 929-9108